THE MYST PHARAOH'S DIAMONDS

AVA & CAROL DETECTIVE AGENCY

THOMAS LOCKHAVEN
WITH EMILY CHASE

TWISTED KEY
publishing

2018

First Printing: 2018

ISBN 978-1-947744-12-7

Twisted Key Publishing, LLC
www.twistedkeypublishing.com

Ordering Information:
Special discounts are available on quantity purchases by corporations, associations, educators, and others. For details, contact the publisher at the above listed address.

U.S. trade bookstores and wholesalers: Please contact Twisted Key Publishing, LLC by email twistedkeypublishing@gmail.com.

CONTENTS

1
THE SCIENTIFIC BURRITO

Ava woke up annoyed at the world. She blew a wet strand of hair from the corner of her mouth.

"Gross," Ava cringed as she peeled her vibrating phone off her cheek. It made a wet suctioning sound like sweaty legs on a leather sofa.

"Ava," a voice chirped. "Time for breakfast."

Ava took in a deep breath, held it for a moment, then sighed dramatically. *How could anyone be so chipper this early?* She rolled out of bed, landing with a heavy thud, taking her blankets with her.

"You alright up there?" her mother called up the stairs.

"Fine!" Ava shouted.

She rolled across the room, successfully wrapping herself into a blanket burrito. Exhausted from the effort, Ava lay motionless on the floor for a moment, staring at her ceiling. She was compelled into motion by the seductive smell of bacon. Still swaddled, she scooched out her bedroom, across the hall to the top of the stairs. She was about to descend à la bobsled when her mother rounded the corner.

Clearly, she had some type of disaster prevention sixth sense… or an anti-fun gene. Maybe both. "What on earth are you doing? Have you lost your mind?"

"I'm rehearsing for a school play. The 'Cocoon That Could,' a poignant story of a butterfly—"

"Ava," her mother's face tightened.

"Fine. It's for a science project. You don't want to impede scientific progress, do you?"

"How about you choose a project that doesn't end up with you in the hospital in a body cast."

"Mom, be reasonable," chuckled Ava. "We don't get to choose science—it chooses us. You married a scientist. Surely, of all people, you should understand."

"Ava Clarke." Her mother's voice took on a much crisper tone. It was followed by the look that only a mother can give.

"Alright," Ava sighed. She shrugged her way out of her blankets, knotted them up in a ball and threw them onto her bed. Science would have to wait—at least until her parents went to work.

Ava crossed the kitchen, turned on the faucet and washed her hands.

"Here," said her mom, handing her a mixing bowl. "Make yourself useful."

Ava ran her finger along the inside of the bowl and licked the pancake batter off her finger. "Tasty."

As she scrubbed the bowl, she leaned forward and gazed out the window. The tiny town of Livingston was alive with activity. People were fetching their newspapers, walking their dogs, breathing in the fresh September air. Ava decided that she would give the morning another chance, and perhaps, even smile.

"Good morning," Ava's dad said through a yawn as he shuffled into the kitchen. He ran his hand through his thick curly brown hair and plopped into a chair at the kitchen table.

"Good morning, Father," Ava said brightly, drying her hands on a dishtowel.

"Morning Aves," he said, stifling another yawn.

"Late night? Doing sciency things?"

"Yep. The CDC sent me a fascinating report last night that they wanted me to review—amazing reading."

Ava's father was a highly sought-after biologist. She was pretty sure the Center of Disease Control had him on speed dial. "I too tried to venture into the world of science this morning. A little *Physics* experiment, but it was quashed by the department of safety and boredom," Ava gestured to her mother.

"Your daughter was attempting to slalom down the stairs wrapped in blankets," explained Mrs. Clarke.

Charles coughed into his hand. Ava could see a tiny smile forming at the edges of his mouth. "You gotta be careful, Aves. Who else is going to look after your mom and I when we're old and senile?"

A *tap, tap* at the door rescued Ava from answering. "We'll have to continue this discussion later. Friendship knocketh, and I simply can't allow it to wait."

Carol Miller, Ava's best friend stood on the porch, looking as if she were about to burst with excitement.

Her eyes sparkled like crystal blue marbles in the sunlight.

"Did you hear? Tell me you heard," said Carol, shaking Ava by the shoulders.

"That you are insane? Yes, come in. My parents have already scheduled an intervention. My mother is burning sage and chanting as we speak."

"Do you ever check your phone? The Hancock Museum was robbed last night!"

Ava hesitated a beat. "Are you serious? What's there to steal?"

Carol let out an exasperated puff of air. "Hello? Ramesses exhibit on loan to our museum from Egypt ring a bell?" asked Carol, following Ava to the kitchen.

"Big brain just said the Hancock Museum was robbed." Carol nodded in agreement.

"I knew something like this was going to happen," said Mrs. Clarke. Ava shot her mom a quizzical look. "The security at the museum…," she shook her head. "Don't even get me started."

"My dad said they updated the entire security system and even built a *safe room* that was approved by an Egyptian dignitary," explained Carol.

"You never told me about that," said Ava.

"My dad's an architect. He's done work for just about everyone in town. The museum was just another job."

"The only reason the Hancock Museum was even allowed to host the exhibit was because Eugene McDunnel—the philanthropist that bankrolled the original Egyptian expedition—his grandson lives here in Livingston," added Mrs. Clarke.

"That's amazing," said Carol. "History makes me swoon."

"'Destined to Be Alone,' the title of a book I'm writing about Carol's life, in case anyone's interested."

"I interviewed Mr. McDunnel for the New Yorker. After it's run here, the exhibit was to go to the Metropolitan Museum of Art in November."

"They just announce where an exhibit is going?" asked Ava. "Seems counterintuitive as far as keeping priceless artifacts safe."

"Look at you, throwing around the five syllable words."

"Thank you, Carol. Contrary to popular belief, I happen to have a massive vocabulary. I simply don't know the meaning of half the words."

"They *have* to announce it to the public, Ava. Museums get a lot of publicity and money by offering exhibitions like this," Charles blew across the rim of his coffee and took a sip. "I would have thought that Hancock Museum would have learned a lesson after what happened to the Isabella Stewart Gardner Museum in 1990."

"Okay, that's oddly specific," said Ava.

"It's the biggest art heist in history," explained Mrs. Clarke. "Thieves dressed up as police officers. They told the security guards that someone had reported a disturbance. The guards let them in, and the crooks stole thirteen paintings worth over 500 million dollars."

"Were they ever caught?" Carol inquired.

"No, the FBI never caught them," said Mrs. Clarke. "I've actually written quite a bit about art heists. The unfortunate thing is eighty percent of them go unsolved."

"Eighty percent?" Ava stroked her chin thoughtfully. "If I ever decide to go into a life of crime, it's going to be robbery." Her parents stared at her mortified. "What?" Ava asked innocently. "Look at the benefits—there's only a twenty-percent chance that you'd have to bail me out."

"I'm sure they'll catch whoever robbed the museum. There are literally cameras everywhere. It's not like they can just walk into an airport with—wait, what did they steal?"

"A sarcophagus," teased Ava.

Ava's mom made several swipes on her phone. "It says that five diamonds were stolen, valued at twenty-million dollars. Carol's right though—they can't just hop on a plane with millions of dollars' worth of diamonds."

"So, what's the use of stealing them? Who are they going to sell them to?"

"My guess is they'll either try to sneak them out of the country somehow and sell them to a private collector, or they'll begin negotiations with the insurance company that is insuring them."

"Why would they talk to the insurance company? 'We've got your diamonds. We promise we won't hurt them. Let's make a deal.'"

"You're not too far off," laughed Mrs. Clarke. "They'll negotiate with the insurance company for a few million. The insurance company will agree to an amount, and they'll anonymously make the trade."

"Sounds like a rip off. But…," Ava conceded, "it's better to pay a few million for something worth twenty million than to not have it at all."

"I'm sorry to interrupt," said Carol. "This is fascinating. Really it is. But the bus is going to be here in about two minutes."

Ava shoveled several forkfuls of pancakes in her mouth and hurried over to the refrigerator. She grabbed a Juicebox for herself and one for Carol, then hurried across the kitchen and slung on her backpack.

"See you guys this afternoon!" yelled Ava over her shoulder as she rushed for the door. Carol smiled and waved to Ava's parents as she followed close on her friend's heels.

2
RAMESSES'S CURSE

The final bell rang, turning the school hallway into a miniature version of the running of the bulls. In full stampede, children hooted and hollered as they pushed their way out of the six bright red doorways leading to freedom. A semicircle of buses arced around Nobel Park Middle School like a bright orange smiley face.

Carol and Ava blinked as their eyes adapted to the brilliant sun, which instantly warmed them. Carol closed her eyes and turned her face upward. "Ah, this is the life," she sighed.

Ava looked at the buses, their diesel exhaust puffing like cigars. "What do you say we walk home today?"

Carol sighed pleasantly. "Please! I just want to fling my arms out and run through a wheat field or grove of wildflowers."

"What about a field of corn instead… could you imagine? Thud, thud, thud as you plow down an entire crop of corn. You'd have serious welts all over your arm."

"Why do you do that? Do you have something against pleasant thoughts? You just destroyed a perfect moment of heavenly bliss," moaned Carol. She paused and stretched out her arms once again, trying to regain the blissful moment. "Nope, you ruined it. It's gone," she let her arms drop to her sides.

"Speaking of bliss," said Ava, stopping at a crosswalk, "how did you do on the geography test?"

Carol frowned as they crossed Elm Street and continued down the sidewalk, heading toward Mall Street. "Sadly, there was no test today. Mr. Downey decided the museum heist was more important than the globe."

"Tragic."

"I agree. He wanted to share his theory on how the robbery was committed and how the thieves got away."

"I'm afraid to ask... but somehow, I feel compelled."

"He thinks that it was Ramesses himself that stole the diamonds. He believes that Ramesses couldn't go onward to the afterlife because he had unfinished business," Carol wiggled her fingers mysteriously.

"In Livingston...," added Ava.

"Of course," snorted Carol. "He's also the same teacher who said that we never landed on the moon, that everything was filmed on a soundstage in Hollywood."

"I unfortunately stumbled onto his YouTube channel where he shot a video to debunk the moon landing. I must say, he takes his videography very seriously. For authenticity, he shot his video in his daughter's sandbox."

"Geez," muttered Carol under her breath. "I hope he doesn't have a cat. That's one lunar landing I wouldn't want to see."

"We're educationally doomed," laughed Ava. "You have to admit, the robbery is the biggest thing that's happened in Livingston."

"Do I? You're forgetting the alien baby in the Charles River."

"Oh yeah, the one that turned out to be an octopus that got its tentacles oddly twisted in a plastic six-pack ring thingy."

"We made the front page of the *National Enquirer* with that one," Carol said matter-of-factly. "Our one fleeting moment of fame and then back into dismal obscurity."

"That was funny," said Ava. "Remember people swore they saw a saucer-shaped spaceship crash into the river just hours before the *octo-alien* appeared?"

"What can I say?" Carol said. "Peeps are gullible and clueless."

Ava nodded, agreeing with her friend. "Speaking of clueless, without looking, what am I wearing?"

"Oh Ava, Ava, you must think you're dealing with a neophyte."

"I'm going to let that one pass because I have no idea what that is. I can only assume that it means possessing godlike qualities."

"Exactly, I promise you that it doesn't mean inexperienced or beginner."

"You're a horrible liar. So…," Ava prompted.

"A large yellow hat with a wide brim, a yellow poncho and galoshes. You may or may not have a mustache."

"Great, you're amazing. You just described the guy that does the fish-sticks commercial."

"Fine. You no longer have red highlights, you have purple. You're wearing your black hoodie that has the word 'ironic' stenciled on it, but no one can see the word ironic because it is stenciled in black."

"It's classic," interjected Ava.

"Let's see, you're wearing jeans and your black converse with the purple shoelaces to accentuate your new highlights. You have purple nail polish on every finger except your ring finger."

The girls came to a stop at the corner and waited as a black SUV with a reinforced grill, tinted windows and multiple antennas sped past.

"Not a part of the Livingston police department," said Carol, eyeing the government license plate.

"Mom said that they brought in the FBI on the art heist in Boston—it makes sense they would be here for this one."

The girls jogged across the intersection to the sidewalk that ran along Mall Street.

"I was thinking about something my mom said."

Carol stopped and leaned against Mr. Gupter's mailbox. "Alright, I see the wheels churning."

"The thief—"

"Or thieves," added Carol.

Ava nodded and continued, "They have *two* options to get rid of the diamonds. One is to sell them to the insurance company and the second was to smuggle them out of the country."

"They don't necessarily have to smuggle them out of the country, especially if they sell them to a private dealer who wants them as an ego purchase."

"Which would you choose? Would you risk working with an insurance company? I mean, there's gonna be some kind of digital footprint, right? You're gonna leave tracks."

"Most likely. It depends on how computer savvy the person is. Remember, our computer club hacked into a bunch of local businesses as a part of *operation safety net* to show how unsecure they were."

"Exactly. You may be a great thief, but that doesn't mean you have the computer skills to communicate with an insurance company and not leave a trace. Plus, you also have to have knowledge of overseas banking. It's not like they're going to mail you a check."

Carol snorted, "'Yes, uhm… if you would please make the check out to Ima. Ima Robber.'"

"I feel so conflicted. Robbers have to be trustworthy. Think about it. If you have accomplices…."

"Cohorts."

THE MYSTERY OF THE PHARAOH'S DIAMONDS | 13

"Yeah, that's a better word… you have to trust that they're not going to double-cross you, or that they have the necessary skills to do all the stuff that needs to get done."

"Takes a lot of planning," agreed Carol.

"And how do you find these people? Is there like a website with a drop-down menu where you can select the type of criminal you need?"

"Sort of… it's called the dark web." Ava gave Carol a look. "I don't have all the answers," she shrugged, "just enough to make it look like I know what I'm talking about."

"Honestly, I'm betting the diamonds are probably halfway across the globe by now. Even with all the cameras and technology, it would be simple to hop on a train, or boat with them. Plus, the thieves had months to plan. Right now, everyone's playing catch-up."

"I agree."

"I also noticed we walked by my house about five minutes ago," said Ava.

"Eh, you're right," Carol smiled, reversing directions. "I believe I got confused by all the smoke coming from your ears."

"So clever. Maybe next time, try a joke from this century," Ava laughed, bumping shoulders with Carol.

"This robbery reminds me of the great clock heist we solved."

"Oh yeah!" exclaimed Ava. "When Connor and Talon stole all the clocks from the classrooms and sold them on that website where schools request items at a discount in bulk."

"Catching them was our one true moment to shine."

"I loved your article about it in the *Cherrywood Chatter*. 'It's Time for Justice to Prevail.' So how did that story remind you of the robbery?"

"It didn't really. I just felt like reliving the moment. The adulation from our peers, the pats on the back, the reward money."

"I did enjoy the adulation, and the free tacos," said Ava as they walked up her driveway. "Carol, when was the last time you visited the Hancock Museum?"

Carol smiled, her blue eyes sparkling. "Why Mrs. Clarke, are you inviting me on a mission?"

"I believe I am Big Brain. I believe I am."

3
THE BLOODY BRAIN

"Carol and I have decided to solve the museum robbery."

Ava's mom pushed her glasses on top of her head and massaged her temples. "I think the FBI and local police have that covered. However, if you feel like using your deductive reasoning, you could solve the mystery of who keeps leaving their dirty clothes all over your floor."

"Pfft," Ava waved her comment aside. "As an intrepid journalist, I thought that you would be more supportive. We have solved numerous crimes."

Carol held up two fingers.

"Ava, I know that it's your thing to try and fix everything, but sometimes it takes a certain… skillset that comes with practice and time. You wouldn't want to go in for surgery from a mechanic, would you?"

"Depends, some refer to the human body as nature's engine."

"No one refers to the human body as nature's engine," Carol grimaced. "That sounds just *awful*."

"What if it's a surgeon that moonlights as a mechanic?"

"Ava, you don't know the first thing about carrying on an investigation. You have to build up your investigative chops, and that takes a while. Most people find mentors to help guide them."

"That's where you're wrong, Mom. I've been immersed in detective work for over a decade."

"Really? You were *immersed* in detective work since you were two?" Mrs. Clarke folded her arms.

"You told me that you and Dad used to watch *Law & Order* when you were pregnant with me. Suffice to say, I learned quite a bit at a young impressionable age."

Ava's mom sighed. "Why do I even bother? I think the FBI has everything under control. Plus, they've learned a lot since the Isabella robbery."

"I guess you're right, Mom. I don't know what I was thinking."

"Ava," said her mom softly. She stood and wrapped her arms around her daughter. "It's wonderful to have a curious mind and that you want to help. I'm proud of you."

"Thanks. I get it, Carol and I need more practice. Start small but aim high." Ava's mom squeezed her hard, then returned to her desk where there were dozens of papers scattered around her laptop.

"Well, we'll leave you to your work." Ava motioned for Carol to follow her into the kitchen. She grabbed two bowls from the cabinet and grabbed a carton of Ninja Chip Ice cream. *Ice cream, so sneaky, you'll never see the calories coming.*

"I'm guessing, you are going to ignore everything your Mom said."

"Yep," said Ava, licking her spoon. "How are you supposed to *get* experience if you're not allowed to practice?"

Carol eyed the kitchen door. "I think we should continue our conversation in a less public venue."

Carol draped herself over Ava's bed, letting her head hang over the edge.

"What are you doing?" laughed Ava.

"Filling my brain with blood—it helps me think better."

"It's certainly attractive." Ava grabbed her laptop from her desk and hopped onto her bed. She flipped her computer open and opened a word document. "This is officially our third case."

"Wonderful. Good things come in threes." Carol pushed herself up and scooched over beside Ava.

"Feel smarter?"

"Indubitably."

"Perfect. We need an official name for this investigation. Our last one, 'Find the Clocks,' was quite uninspired. We need something with pizazz."

"The Missing Diamonds?"

"Do you even hear yourself? That's too generic. Something like 'The Case of the Pharaoh's Diamonds,' or—"

"'The Ramesses Heist,'" suggested Carol.

"'The Ramesses Heist.' I have to say, it rolls off the tongue. 'The Ramesses Heist,'" Ava mouthed as she typed. "So, what do we know so far?"

"Honestly not much," Carol screwed up her face. "We know that five diamonds were stolen. That the robbery occurred while the museum was closed."

"That the museum had a new security system," Ava added. "Oh, that it was a traveling exhibition."

"That the show had an Egyptian security specialist that traveled with the show."

"Good one," said Ava as she typed. "Anything else?"

"Not really. The police and the news haven't been very forthcoming with details."

"What's our hypothesis? By the way, Mrs. Wright would be so proud of us right now. Formulating a hypothesis."

"Hmm," Carol chewed on her bottom lip. "That the thieves knew about the exhibit ahead of time. That they most likely cased the museum and had already established what to do with the diamonds once they stole them, and that at this very moment, they are trying to sneak them out of the country."

"That means time is of the essence," mused Ava. "Especially if the thieves are trying to move the diamonds out of the country." Ava typed the details into the case file.

"If they're trying to smuggle them out of the country, they would have to deal with customs."

"Customs is no joke. Last time we went to Mexico, we had to go through an x-ray machine, and they searched our luggage. I'm pretty sure it's going to be that way no matter where you travel."

"I think we should start at the museum and see if we can find any clues there. We have a half-day at school tomorrow, so we can go right after we get out."

"Perfect! I'll look online tonight and see if I can find out anything else about the heist."

"Me too," said Carol, fishing her phone from her pocket. She swiped a finger across the screen and fired off a text. "I gotta run. Dinner's ready."

"Okay." Ava hopped up off the bed and slipped her shoes on. "Let me know if you find anything."

"Will do," said Carol, scrambling down the stairs.

"Oh, one other thought," Ava lowered her voice. "See if your dad can tell you a little bit about the safe room the museum added. You never know what's going to be a clue."

"Good idea."

Ava waited until Carol reached the bottom step before she switched the sprinklers on. She watched as her friend jumped from side to side trying not to get wet. *You always gotta be on your toes*, smiled Ava, closing the front door.

4
THE CRIME SCENE

It was a cloud-free day. The sun was shining brightly, casting a harsh glare off the asphalt as the girls rode their bikes down Main Street. They made a quick stop at Baker's Café, then continued through the center of town toward the museum.

Ava wiped her brow with her forearm, squinting into the oncoming traffic. They hopped off the bikes, and walked them across the crosswalk, coming to a stop at the midnight blue bike racks located in front of the main entrance of the museum.

Ava removed an incredibly small notebook and stub of a pencil from her pocket.

"What, did you rob a Muppet? What's with the tiny pad? Wait, let me guess, you accidentally put it in the dryer."

"You might laugh, but detectives around the world use pads just like this."

"I'm sorry," Carol had the face of someone that had just one more question. "I'm just curious… is there a website that sells tiny things?"

"Yes, I believe it's where your parents got your brain."

"Lashing out. That's how it's going to be."

"You mess with the tools of the trade, and you get knocked down a notch or two." Ava ran her fingers through her helmet hair. "Plus, I know that you're just acting out of jealousy. I pity you."

"Alright. Alright." Carol threw up her hands in surrender. "You caught me. I'm obsessed with your tiny notepad. I wonder if they used a bonsai to make it. You know… because they're so small."

Ava pursed her lips. "You know what? I have half a mind not to give this to you." Ava reached in her back pocket and removed an equally small notepad and pencil for Carol.

Carol's jaw dropped. "You got me a mini pad too?" She let out a low whistle as she examined it. "I take back everything I said."

"That's what I thought," said Ava. "I've jotted down a couple notes for us."

"Did you write them in shorthand? I'm sorry, I can't stop myself."

"May I continue?" Carol nodded and drew her fingers across her lips as if she was zipping them shut. Ava glanced around to make sure no one was within earshot. "Currently, I've only written three directives. One, investigate the museum. Two, question suspects. Three, froyo."

"Impressive. Clandestine stuff right there. Glad no one overheard you."

"Jealousy will consume you until there's nothing left." Ava put her hand on Carol's shoulder. "You'll be an empty husk. Ask yourself, do you want to be an empty husk?"

"I'm going to go in there," said Carol, pointing to the museum, "to start the investigation. If you want, we can stop by the library on the way home, and I'll get you a book on Socrates."

The Hancock Museum was one of Livingston's oldest landmarks, built over two hundred years ago. The museum had gone through numerous expansions and renovations. The walls were like a patchwork of Livingston history, made of a collage of different colored stones and bricks from the past and present.

Carol placed her hand over her eyes, shading her face from the afternoon sun as they climbed the steps to the entrance. "Do your three directives have to be done in any specific order?"

"Yes, they need to be followed, step by step. Why?"

"I'm so thirsty, and Fro-to-Go is pulling on my soul like a tractor beam."

"Froyo comes last because it will be our reward for a job well done."

"Fine," muttered Carol as she pushed open the glass door that led into the museum. The girls paused in the doorway as a wave of A/C kissed their red faces.

"I've just died and gone to arctic heaven," moaned Ava. She delighted in the chill running from the nape of her neck to the soles of her feet.

"You go ahead," said Carol. "I'll guard the entrance to make sure no one escapes."

"Ahem. May I help you?"

If Mother Nature had a voice, thought Carol, *this is it!* Ava and Carol looked up to see an elderly lady with the kindest blue-gray eyes they had ever seen. She stood behind a gray circular workstation, staring at them.

"Good morning," smiled Carol. "How are you?"

"I'm wonderful. How may I help you?" The older woman had a delightful singsong voice.

"We would like two tickets, please." Carol pulled out a twenty-dollar bill.

"That will be sixteen dollars," smiled the old woman.

Ava noticed a small glass box labeled "Donations." "Can you please put the change in the donation box?" asked Ava, smiling sweetly.

"Thank you," said the woman. "That is very kind of you."

"You're welcome," beamed Ava.

"Do you need a map? We have several new exhibits. Unfortunately, our Egyptian exhibit is currently closed due to... uhm... extenuating circumstances."

"No, ma'am," smiled Ava. "We heard about the robbery. We're here to show our support." Ava looked around the lobby and smiled. "It's been a while. Grandpa Clarke used to bring me here all the time. He had a fascination with trains."

"Oh, wait a moment, are you William Clarke's granddaughter?"

"Yes, ma'am," said Ava, a little unsure. "Grandpa didn't annoy you, did he? I've been told that us Clarkes can be quite annoying. I'm attempting to start a new generation of non-annoying Clarkes."

"Oh my, no! William was a great man," said the woman, beaming. "Yes, your grandfather was very interested in trains. He actually helped build the railroad exhibit on the second floor."

"Wow! He never told me that," said Ava, amazed. "I knew he always loved to spend time in that section, but he never told me he helped build it."

"He was a very sweet and humble man." She smiled and paused for a moment, thinking. "We all miss him *very* much," she said as she patted Ava's hand. Ava blushed, not really sure what to say. "Well," she cleared her throat, "enough of an old woman's ramblings. You're actually just in time— the elementary school will be here soon. You should get some quality viewing time before they arrive."

"Thank you for the heads-up," winked Ava.

"Enjoy your visit."

"Thank you so much…," Carol hesitated as she glanced down at the woman's name tag, "Gladys. I'm Carol and—"

"I'm Ava," Ava piped in.

"Well, it's a pleasure to meet both of you! If you have any questions, please let me know."

"We will," the girls said in unison.

As soon as the girls were out of earshot, Carol turned to Ava. "Did you see the way she looked when she talked about your grandfather?"

Ava nodded, "I'm beginning to think grandpa had more on his mind than trains, if you know what I mean," Ava giggled.

They passed by an office that read "Administration" and then another marked "Security". The door swung open just as the girls reached the stairwell. A tall guard slipped out the door and jogged up the stairs ahead of them. Ava and Carol had just enough time to peek in the door and see another guard leaning back in a chair, staring at a bank of monitors.

"Security," Carol made a face. "That's one job I would not want to have right now."

"No kidding," Ava whispered. "I wonder why they keep that sign up," she pointed to a sprawling, bright red banner that hung twenty feet above their heads— it read "King Ramesses's Secrets—Egyptian Exhibit. August 21– 31."

"It's like a constant reminder of what you've lost."

"Mom said the Isabella museum keeps the empty frames of the stolen paintings hanging, as a placeholder for when they return home."

"That's both hopeful and sad," said Carol.

THE MYSTERY OF THE PHARAOH'S DIAMONDS | 27

"Agreed," nodded Ava.

The girls followed the stairs to the second floor where a small sign with an arrow said: "Ramesses Exhibit—Bowyer Hall".

"I don't see anyone up here," whispered Carol, her head swiveling back and forth.

"Bummer. I was kind of hoping we could blend in with the crowd," said Ava.

The brightly lit hallway was split up into four different sections: Early American Indian Artifacts, Livingston Railway System, History of Livingston, and the Ramesses Exhibit. The room for the Ramesses exhibit was dark, and several strips of yellow and black police tape crisscrossed over the entrance to the room.

Security cameras scrutinized everyone who walked down the hallway, every second of every day—which presented a problem for the girls. How were they supposed to get into the Egyptian exhibit and search for clues if it was blocked off and monitored?

"Do you think those cameras are on?" asked Ava, who raised her eyes upward without moving her head. "I don't see a little red light like in the movies."

"I'm sure they are," said Carol, "especially after the robbery."

"That's true," agreed Ava.

"I have a feeling if we so much as walk down the hallway toward the exhibit, the guards are going to be all over us."

"Can you disable the cameras with your phone? You know like hack into their system?"

"Dude, I'm in the computer club, not the Avengers."

"I see," Ava sighed a heavy sigh filled with disappointment. "We need to get the guards away from the monitors." She gestured to a room named the "History of Livingston." "I have a plan! Follow me."

Carol followed Ava into the exhibit. The walls were filled with grainy black-and-white pictures of Livingston. A huge picture hung in the back of the room, showing a panoramic view of the entire town. Beneath the city streets, the picture showed a complex tunnel system that reminded Carol of an ant farm. The tunnels had been sealed in the 1890s after a series of cave-ins.

"So, what's the plan?" whispered Carol.

Ava didn't respond. She noticed a reflection on the picture's metallic frame. Someone was watching them from the doorway.

"Carol," Ava whispered out of the corner of her mouth, "we're being watched. Pretend to be gaga over these pictures."

"Woah," said Carol as she pointed at the huge black-and-white photography. "Is that Bennett's Groceries? Look, it used to be just a small stand selling vegetables."

"That's incredible!" exclaimed Ava.

"Now it's like a megastore."

"Look at this," said Ava enthusiastically as she pointed to a grainy picture. "The Livingston Savings and Loan is over 160 years old! How the heck did they get an aerial picture of the bank? They didn't have airplanes back then."

"A tethered hot air balloon," said a friendly, deep male voice.

Ava and Carol whirled around. A short, robust security guard stood in the doorway. He had a scruffy patch of reddish-brown hair and equally red cheeks. He looked like he had just finished running a race. He walked from his belly as if being pulled by a rope. Heave-ho.

"This picture is from the year 1860," he said. "They raised a hot air balloon to nearly a hundred feet." He raised his hand in the air as if it were a hot air balloon. "And then they tied it to a large oak tree, right here in the front of the museum. Here's a photograph of the hot air balloon," the guard pointed at another picture. "Aerial photography was cutting-edge technology back then. The big photograph of the city is actually a series of eight photographs all stitched together to make one big picture."

"That's incredible," said Carol as she looked back toward the picture. "I never realized that so many of the businesses in the picture are actually still around."

"Many of the businesses in Livingston are still run by the same family."

"They used hot air balloons in battle?" asked Ava, reading the placard beneath the photograph. "Seems a little risky."

"They sure did. They used them during the Civil War to spy on enemy troops."

"Kind of like we use drones now," said Carol.

"Exactly! The soldiers were incredibly resourceful. Did you know they ran telegraph wires from the balloons, so they could get real-time information to the commanding officers on the battlefield? History is fascinating!" the guard beamed.

"Thank you," said Ava, "you're like a walking computer." She smiled at the guard.

"Thank you," he smiled back. "I'll take that as a compliment."

Carol and Ava moved slowly around the room. They were running out of things to talk about, and they were worried that the guard was going to be a permanent shadow. They were just about to run out of *oohs* and *ahhs* when a voice began jabbering from the security guard's earpiece.

"Please, please, please," whispered Carol.

The guard stepped out of the doorway and spoke quietly. Ava glanced at Carol—her fingers crossed. Good fortune must like crossed fingers because the guard's next words were "I'm on my way." They looked at each other and let out a joint sigh of relief—*finally*!

They pretended not to notice that the guard had left the room in case he checked back in on them—and only when they heard his footsteps descending the stairs did they relax.

"OK, quickly, before he comes back," said Ava. "I've got to get into the Egyptian room."

"How? In case you forgot, there are two cameras. There is no way into that room without them seeing you."

"Well, actually there is. You just have to think outside the box," smiled Ava.

"If your plan involves me being grounded for the rest of my life, I swear to you I will shave your eyebrows and knit the world's smallest sweater," Carol warned.

Ava, despite herself and the seriousness of the situation, snorted. "I promise you that you won't be grounded for the rest of your life. My plan is infallible—there is no way we'll get caught."

Carol tapped her wrist as if pointing to an imaginary watch. "Alright, give me the info before the human shadow returns."

"Here's my plan. When we came upstairs, there was a room marked 'Security.' You saw it, right?"

"Of course...," said Carol, already scrunching up her face.

"I need you to bang on that door, and when the guard comes to the door, I need you to tell him that you ate a day-old egg salad sandwich from a gas station and that you have to find a restroom, pronto. Trust me, people will move mountains to get you to a restroom. No one messes with old egg salad."

"*Trust* is the last thought that is coming to my mind right now…," said Carol warily.

"Listen, I just need the guard to be away from the video monitors for ten seconds," Ava said. "That'll give me enough time to get into the room without being seen."

"You've lost your mind," said Carol. "How are you going to get out of the room when you're done? You want me to run back to the security room five minutes later and tell him there's no TP too?"

"Hmmm," said Ava, stroking her chin with her index finger and thumb. "That's not a bad idea."

"There's one small problem with your plan—how are you going to know when the guard comes to the door?" asked Carol.

"Problem? There's no problem—that is actually the easiest part."

Carol met Ava's eyes with a look of unquestionable doubt, or a look of impending doom—Ava couldn't really tell.

"You have your phone, right?" inquired Ava.

"Yes," said Carol cautiously.

"Well, call me now, and then put your phone in your pocket. I'll be able to hear what's going on. Easy peasy."

"I'm going to look like an absolute idiot banging on the security door," moaned Carol.

"Really? Is this the voice of a seasoned journalist? I thought the *Cherrywood Chatter* was a paper that stood for—"

"All right, all right, I'll do it!"

"Okay," said Ava, holding her friend's shoulders, looking deep into her eyes. "Let me see that look."

"Um, what look?" asked Carol, confused and annoyed.

"Come on, the *I gotta go* look!"

"If we live through this, I'm taking you to counseling—you truly need help." Carol pulled her phone out of her pocket and hit Ava's name. Ava felt her phone vibrate. "I'm changing your name to traitor," Carol hissed.

"You don't mean that," said Ava, putting her hands on Carol's shoulders who shrugged away. "Oh, tuna works too. Old tuna—there's nothing worse."

Carol turned and walked away. Ava could hear the muffled *swoosh, swoosh* of her jeans as she walked down the stairs. Ava stood just inside the doorway of the exhibit so the security cameras couldn't see her, her heart pounding in her chest.

Just a short distance away, as Carol descended the stairs, she pondered her life choices.

The swooshing stopped. Suddenly, Ava heard *bang, bang, bang* as Carol pounded on the security door. Seconds later, she heard a buzz, and then a very angry male voice.

Hmm, I didn't need the phone after all. Ava didn't hang around to hear what they said. She snuck a peek out the doorway, bolted down the hall, and dove under the police tape into the Ramesses Exhibit. She slid across the room, coming to a stop at the base of a sarcophagus. Her softball coach would have been proud.

Ava stood up, brushed her leggings off, and peeled a long strip of police tape from her forehead. A huge smile spread across her face. She'd made it!

The Egyptian exhibit room was richly decorated. Strips of sunlight painted thin, vertical lines across the room. *Yeesh, this room is creepy,* thought Ava as she slowly turned in a circle.

At the far side of the room stood a huge wooden sarcophagus, encased in glass. The placard beneath it read "Ramesses II—Ruler of Egypt 1279 BC–1213 BC." The walls were covered with pictures of all shapes and sizes of pyramids, burial sites, and Egyptian gods. A replica of the Rosetta stone, sat against the side wall. *Wow, those language CDs have been around forever!*

A decorative gold stand stood in the middle of the room. The top spread out like fingers to support an incredibly thick glass housing that was supposed to protect the pharaoh's diamonds.

A circle, about the size of a grapefruit, had been cut into the top of the glass enclosure. Ava could see some kind of brownish, yellow oil around the edges of the circle. She pulled out her phone and started taking pictures. The glass enclosure was over an inch thick, and a series of massive bolts had been drilled through the glass into the stand. It was securely anchored to the floor by eight more bolts.

Okay, so they used a glass cutter to steal the diamonds. But how did they get in? Would they be brazen enough to just sneak past the guards? Did they come in through the loading zone?

Ava looked up at the corner of the room. A motion detector flashed. Her heart jumped, *why didn't it go off?* She cautiously moved toward it. There appeared to be something over the sensor. It looked like a thick piece of glass, the size of a matchbook.

Ava then eyed the window. Both locks were secured. An alarm with a digital readout sat atop the window frame. It sent millions of invisible pulses to a receiver—if the connection was broken, the alarm would go off. *I don't see any scratches on the locks or any sign of forced entry.* But, Ava noticed, the center of the windowsill was clean, whereas the outer edges had dust on them, as if the center had been wiped down.

Ava took a picture of the window, the locks, and the alarm system. She peered down—it was at least a twenty-five-foot drop from the window to the ground. She spun around and took pictures of the motion detector. *Mental note, the thieves had to have visited the exhibit earlier—there has to be video of them. Figure out how to see the video.*

Just as she was about to take a panoramic video of the room, an angry voice shouted, "What are you doing in there?!"

Ava nearly jumped out of her skin. A very vexed and very muscular security guard stood in the doorway, holding Carol by the top of her arm. Ava recognized him from the security room. He had jet-black hair and barely visible beady little eyes that at the moment, Ava knew, were boring holes into her soul. His walrus-sized mustache would've been funny, but under the circumstances, even his mustache looked frightening.

"You're not supposed to be in there!" he yelled, his face contorted and turned an unhealthy crimson color. "You are trespassing and breaking the law." He jabbed his finger at the police tape.

Ava gulped, her mind was spinning, how was she going to get them out of this one? Carol just stood with her head hanging low, looking like a broken puppet.

"Get out of there right now!" he demanded, pointing an accusatory finger at Ava.

"I'm going, I'm going." Ava considered her options. She could either try running and jumping over the tape, limbo beneath it, or—she decided on the least confrontational method. Ava dropped to her hands and knees and crawled under the police tape. As she stood, all she saw was leg and more leg. *Geez, he's tall.*

The man looked from Ava to Carol and then back to Ava. "What were you doing in that room?" he looked at Ava suspiciously. "And don't try to play games with me! I'm a human lie detector."

"I apologize, I was taking a selfie. Carol and I are into true crime shows, and I accidentally dropped my phone. It slid into the room."

The man stuck out his lower lip and scowled. "I told you, don't *lie* to me." He squeezed Carol's arm, making her wince.

Ava went from being frightened to infuriated. "Let go of her right now. You do realize she's the mayor's daughter, you jerk!" bluffed Ava.

The guard looked taken aback for a moment, and then regained his composure. He lowered his snarling face toward Ava.

She took a step back. He definitely wasn't a fan of mouthwash.

"The mayor is in her eighties. I highly doubt this is her daughter."

"Did I say daughter? I meant granddaughter. You're going to be in so much trouble."

"Her granddaughter cut the ribbon for our new exhibit. She's forty years old."

"Really, then my friend here has been lying to me this whole time. I'm not judging you Carol but pretending to be the mayor's granddaughter." Ava shook her head. "If you are finished accosting my friend, I'll make sure she gets the help that she needs."

Carol shook her head. *I'm so going to kill her.*

"Matter of fact, I should capture this moment." Ava held up her phone and snapped a picture. "You couldn't capture the culprit behind the theft, but you managed to grab a teenage girl."

"That does it. Give me your phone." He grabbed Ava by the hand and proceeded to try to rip it from her. Ava clamped her other hand on top of the phone, squeezing it like an anaconda. The guard grabbed her index finger and pried it backward.

"Ouch!" yelled Ava. Without a thought, she whirled toward the guard and slammed her foot into his shin.

The guard's throat made a weird squeaky noise and his eyes nearly bulged out of his skull. "Yee ouch!" he screamed, even more enraged than before.

Ava's mouth also flew open as stars danced in front of her eyes. She'd seen dozens of kids kick bad guys in the shins, but no one had warned her that it was a toe-crushing experience. She had been led to believe that it was the ultimate bad guy escape trick. Sadly, she had been deceived by Hollywood.

"Ow! Just ow!" she breathed out, walking in circles. Her toes began sending the word ouch over and over to her brain, followed by the heartfelt question of "Why? What did we do to deserve this?"

The guard's face had turned from crimson to a lovely shade of purple. It was as if he had the ability to channel all the colors of the rainbow, or a bag of skittles. He lunged at Ava just as a heavenly voice, like a ray of sunlight, broke through the chaos.

"George Marcel! What on earth are you doing?!" The security guard whipped his head around. He immediately released Ava's hand and let go of Carol's arm.

"What is going on here? Have you lost your mind?!" Gladys's voice rang out powerfully.

Ava and Carol couldn't believe it—Gladys had come to their rescue. They looked at each other and then at George.

"Gladys, I caught this young lady snooping around the Egyptian exhibit. The police said *no one* was to go into that room under *any* circumstances." He looked darkly at the girls. "I think they should be in jail!"

"George, they are children. I hardly think the police are going to arrest them and haul them off to jail. I know that you are under a lot of stress, but really…," she shook her head in disapproval. "I'll take over from here. I know Ava's parents."

She turned to Ava and Carol, her face filled with anger. "Girls," she said sternly, "we are going to go downstairs to have a little chat, and then you're calling your parents to tell them what you've done."

George reluctantly agreed. Under the pretense of reattaching a piece of police tape, he kneeled and whispered, "Next time I catch you girls in this museum, I'm going to lock you in the basement." He smiled an evil, villainous smile, then spat out the word "forever."

Ava and Carol shivered as a chill raced down their spines. Carol looked up at Gladys. She could see the disappointment in her eyes, and the tight tug of frustration at the corner of her mouth.

"I'm sorry, Gladys," she whispered.

"We'll talk downstairs," said Gladys as she grasped Carol's hand. "Now help me down these steps."

When they reached Gladys's desk, Ava looked her in the eyes. "I'm so sorry that I went into the exhibit. We heard about the robbery, and we thought maybe we could help."

"I know it seems silly," offered Carol, "but we have solved a couple of cases. Well, not cases, we're not detectives or anything."

Gladys crossed her arms and shook her head. "Girls, I expected more of you. I am incredibly disappointed in your careless, reckless behavior today. This isn't how you go about things."

Ava nearly choked on her words. She had never truly disappointed anyone before and never been called careless or reckless. Okay, not this week. Still, it hurt to see Gladys so disappointed, she'd rather her be angry or furious.

"I'm so sorry," Ava stammered, "Getting into the room, was my idea, not Carol's. My mom's a journalist and she told us about the Isabella robbery, and how eighty percent of art heists go unsolved—I just thought with odds like that, maybe we could help."

"I guess we should have thought things through a little more," whispered Carol, trying to support her friend.

"Yes, you should have," said Gladys with a nod. "If I hadn't been here, George would have certainly called the police and you two would be talking to them right now, not me. However…," she said with a mischievous smile, "I'm always here, and since I *did* rescue you from George, you've gotta tell me if you figured out anything."

"What?" asked Carol, confused. "Aren't you going to call our parents and tell them they've raised a pair of hardened criminals?"

"No," chuckled Gladys, "but I am going to say this: As detectives, you have to take risks, however, you need to figure out if the outcome is going to outweigh the consequences."

"I get it," said Carol. "We're still pretty new at this."

"So," said Gladys. She laced her fingers together and placed them on the counter in front of her, "Tell me everything you know."

"I haven't had enough time to write everything down, so I'll give you a summary of what I found."

"I'm all ears," smiled Gladys. "Seriously, your ears never stop growing, I figure by time I'm ninety I'll be able to fly to work. Like Dumbo."

Ava and Carol snickered. "You're officially the coolest ever," laughed Carol.

"Alright, before Gladys steals my thunder, here's what I found at the crime scene. Actually, you probably know most of this, so let me know if I bore you with the details."

"Well, *I* don't know anything about the exhibit, so you'll be catching me up," said Carol.

"Oh yeah. So, the diamonds were secured in a big glass box that was bolted to the floor. The thieves used a glass cutter to steal the diamonds. There was an oily residue on the glass too." Gladys nodded for her to continue. "I checked to see how the thieves could have gotten in. I know that the museum upgraded the security system. There was a motion detector in the back corner of the room, and the window had a digital alarm as well."

"Did the alarms go off?" asked Carol.

"No," answered Gladys. "The motion detectors are set to alert the alarm company if triggered."

"But they don't go off all the time, so someone has access to whether the alarm is armed or not, right?"

"That is all controlled by the alarm company. Part of the agreement with the Egyptian government was that we would not have the ability to set or reset the motion detectors. They actually hired the company that monitored them."

Ava pulled her phone out of her pocket. "I noticed this attached to the front of the motion detector. It looks like a thick piece of glass, maybe somehow it stopped the sensor from working."

"I'm not sure. Neither the police nor FBI would really give us any details about how the robbery took place."

Carol nodded, "It makes sense—if they suspect someone on the inside, they don't want to give them any information."

"You said the alarm on the window didn't go off, right?"

"Correct," Gladys nodded her head. "The window was locked, and the alarm didn't trigger."

"Oh, because look at this." Ava swiped her finger across the phone. "See how the center of the windowsill is dust-free, and the outer edges are dusty? Like if someone had slid in through the window."

"It's certainly suspicious, but when the police arrived, the window was locked."

"Are there any other entrances into the room?"

"No," Gladys turned from the girls to the front door. A Livingston Elementary School bus had just pulled up in front of the museum. "Sorry, girls. We've only got a minute or two."

"What about video from the cameras? I'm sure the police went through that, right?"

"Oh yes," nodded Gladys. "The police looked at the security video, but on the night of the robbery, there were three hours of video missing. George said that the new online software they use to record the video lost connection and they didn't realize it until hours later."

"How convenient," said Ava.

"Has that ever happened before?" asked Carol curiously.

"Who knows?" said Gladys. "We've never had to test the system. This is our first robbery."

Carol suddenly stiffened. She shouldered Ava. "We're being watched," she whispered. Ava carefully glanced upward, just in time to see someone dart into the shadows.

Gladys shot to her feet and shook an accusatory finger at the girls. "I'm calling each of your parents. You have no business skulking around this museum. Now, instead of calling the police, I want you here twice a week for the next month to clean the lobby and stairs. Is that understood?"

The girls stood, shocked, their mouths hanging open.

"Do you understand?" she demanded.

"Yes… ma'am," they stammered together.

"Good," said Gladys, winking at them, a tiny smile on her face. "Now go home and think about what you've done."

The girls made it through the doors and down the stairs, just as a crowd of children charged the museum.

5
A WINDOW OF OPPORTUNITY

Ava spun on the sidewalk toward Carol. "My heart is still pounding from Gladys's acting. If anyone was watching, it would have definitely fooled them."

"Thank goodness she stepped in when she did," said Carol.

"Yeah, I was about to unleash a world of hurt on him." Carol gave Ava a look, and they both cracked up.

"So," Carol grabbed Ava's hand and they dashed across the crosswalk. "You told Gladys that the windowsill was dust-free in the center."

"Yeah."

"Even though she said the window was locked and the alarm was still set... you think they might have come through the window, don't you?"

"I mean it's a guess. There were only two ways into that room: the main entrance and the window."

Carol nodded in agreement. "I think I know a way we can most likely find out for sure." She gestured toward a small red-and-white awning.

"Livingston Bank?" asked Ava.

"Yes, what do you see?" Carol came to a stop in front of the glass entranceway of the bank.

"I see my reflection…. Oh my God, look at my hair! It looks like I got in a fight with a wind tunnel."

"It's abysmal," laughed Carol. "In the poetic words of the late, great Henry Froodles, it's *hairable*. You have helmet hair," said Carol, running her hand over Ava's head. "It's messy, but it's adorable."

"You just referred to my hair as adorable? Kittens are adorable, puppies are adorable…," Ava shook her head. "This is so humiliating."

"To me, it says, 'Hey, *safety* before *fashion*.' You are a modern-day rebel—embrace it."

Ava wrapped her arms around her shoulders, "I don't feel the love. My seventeen Instagram fans will never forgive me."

"I'm sure they'll get over it. Now, on to more important things."

"Yes, if you would, please explain to me why we are standing in front of the bank."

"So glad you asked. Ava, what is directly across the street from the bank?" inquired Carol.

Ava tilted her head. "Hmm, could it be the museum?"

"Great job," smiled Carol. "And what part of the museum just happens to be facing the bank?"

"The Egyptian exhibit." Ava turned and looked at Carol, amazement filled her face. "Do you think they deposited the diamonds into the bank? Seems so risky."

"What?" asked Carol incredulously. She smacked Ava on the back of the head. "What do ATM's have?"

"Money, and tiny little envelopes for making deposits."

"A camera! You idiot. A camera. They all have cameras," said Carol, jabbing at the camera.

"I know, I know—I was just messing with you, geez…. I make faces at them all the time, hoping that somewhere, some bank manager will be watching the replay and submit my video to an agent in Hollywood."

"At the museum, you were like a bright shooting star," sighed Carol. "And now you implode like a black hole, sucking the very life from my veins." Carol cocked an eyebrow and looked at Ava. "Too much?"

"Yeah, you lost me at the *sucking the very life from my veins part*."

Ava turned and looked at the museum, then turned back to the ATM. "Alright, moving past this awkward moment. We need to see the bank's video from the night of the robbery."

"Bingo," nodded Carol. "You suspect they used the window. Now we just need to see *how*… and if we're lucky, *who*."

"Um, one small hiccup. From what I know about banks, and it's not much, we can't just march into a bank and ask them to show us their security footage.

Plus...," Ava paused, "...I'm sure the police have already done that."

"Lucky for us," said Carol, grabbing the worn brass door handle, "my dad is a good friend of Mr. Talbot, the bank manager."

A small bell jingled as the girls entered the bank. To their right, a row of tellers were busy helping customers. Two small sofas and a couple chairs rested against the opposite wall, and at the far end of the bank were a series of offices.

However, the most alluring piece of furniture was a small pedestal that stood like a gallant knight wedged between the two sofas. Atop the pedestal rested a small ceramic bowl, filled with miniature candy bars and suckers.

Unfortunately, the candy would have to wait. Mr. Talbot was just finishing up with a customer. He made eye contact with Carol and gave her a wink as he said his goodbyes to his customer. Ava cast one quick, mournful look toward the colorful candy treasure that lay just out of reach.

Mr. Talbot was the epitome of dapper. He looked like an older Clark Kent. He wore his hair in a hard part, just above his temple. Eloquent wisps of silver hair—strokes from a master's paintbrush—lay just under the arms of dark-framed, 1960s-style glasses. He wore a perfectly tailored gray suit with a red tie that acted like a punctuation mark to an exquisite outfit.

"Wow," said Ava, looking at Mr. Talbot. "Retro meets modern. I approve."

"Thank you, young lady, and good morning, Carol. To what do I owe this pleasure?" Mr. Talbot asked, smiling down at them.

"Hi, Mr. Talbot. This is my friend, Ava Clarke," she said, gesturing toward Ava.

"Nice to meet you, Ava," he said as he shook her hand. It felt like how a banker's hand should feel. Warm and reassuring.

"Nice to meet you," Ava smiled.

"How are your parents?" he asked, beaming down at Carol. "I haven't seen your dad since we lost the bowling tournament." He paused, balled up his fist, and bit into his knuckles, his manicured nails glistening in the fluorescent lighting. "The Concord Cruisers were exceptional athletes. They tormented us. I was hoping your dad had recovered from the loss…."

Carol patted his arm and nodded her head appreciatively.

"He took it rather hard, Mr. Talbot. He locked himself in his office and threatened to set fire to his favorite bowling shoes—the orange-and-white Dexters…," Carol bowed her head for dramatic effect.

"Not his Dexters," whispered Mr. Talbot, barely audible. "That's horrible. I'll give him a call this evening. The best thing to do after falling off a horse is to get right back on."

"Unless… you have a concussion," said Carol. "Then it's actually best to wait a while, and perhaps seek medical attention."

"Yes," he nodded. "Unless you have a concussion." His eyebrows knotted together, as if they were about to duel. "I apologize, girls. What was it you said you needed?" he asked, looking slightly confused.

"Yes, sorry about that, I'll get right to the point. You of course know about the museum robbery," said Carol.

"Oh, yes, indeed. Nasty business. I'm just glad no one was hurt."

"Well, Ava and I are conducting a little investigation of our own, and I'm writing an article for the school paper, the *Cherrywood Chatter*, about the robbery."

"Oh," said Mr. Talbot, sucking in sharply, his excitement palpable. He leaned in and rested a hand on each girl's shoulder, creating a small huddle of exclusivity. "I used to write for the *Cherrywood Chatter* when I was in school. I was their financial advisor in charge of bake sales, car washes… basically all aspects of fundraising. My articles were as sharp as a tack. My information, though verbose, was filled with financial wisdom. I truly think I made an impact on quite a few of my classmates' lives."

Or helped cure insomnia, thought Ava. Yet, due to her exceptional upbringing, she found herself saying, "Sounds absolutely fascinating."

"Oh, *indeed* it was. Those were the days when writers wrote *real* stories, girls," explained Mr. Talbot, reflecting on the past. "If I hadn't become a banker, I'm sure I would have been a financial reporter, instead of that Elvin Morris on the local news." He gave an exasperated sigh, then looked back at the girls. "I'm sorry, girls. I went off on a tangent. You were asking about the robbery?"

"Don't apologize! I dig your passion, Mr. Talbot," smiled Ava. "It's inspiring." Ava had the rare ability to make just about everyone feel good about themselves. "We were just wondering if the bank's ATM camera records 24/7."

"Oh yes, it certainly does. It's constantly recording, and then that video data is saved to the cloud. I'm not really sure what the cloud is. I always imagine a bunch of computers in a big cloud...," he paused for a second. Ava could tell he was envisioning computers floating on a big, fluffy cumulus cloud. "The video is archived in weekly records," he continued. "I can retrieve the videos from any computer anywhere in the world, as long as I have an internet connection," he smiled proudly.

"Oh cool," said Carol. "So, it basically works like my iPhone. When I save my pics and videos to the cloud, then I can access them later."

"Exactly," smiled Mr. Talbot. "It's not like the old days where everything was stored on tape."

"Do you ever submit any of the ATM videos to the news, or Hollywood agents?" asked Ava. "For example," she explained, "if you were to see, you know, raw talent?" Ava brushed her purple bangs from her forehead and gave him a quick profile.

Mr. Talbot stared at Ava out of the corner of his eye, his forehead wrinkled just slightly. "Um, no… but I'll keep that in mind next time I binge-watch my surveillance videos."

Ava nodded and smiled an upside-down smile. Upside-down smiles were not natural for her. In fact, it was quite difficult, but she had been secretly practicing in her room for such an occasion. She pulled the corners of her mouth downward, flexing her cheek muscles until they ached. She'd seen her mom do it when she talked with other journalists about important stuff, so she had decided to practice the move on Mr. Talbot.

He looked at Ava confused and squinted his eyes just a little. "So…," he continued, "you want to look at the video because you think it shows the robbery?"

"Yes," Carol nodded excitedly.

"I certainly don't mind you looking, but you do realize the ATM camera is facing the side of the museum, not the front."

"Which is perfect," explained Carol. "We think the thieves accessed the Egyptian exhibit via the windows facing the bank."

"Interesting," said Mr. Talbot. "Well, let's get to it. My office is this way and you girls have a robbery to solve."

The girls followed Mr. Talbot through a set of glass doors, down a short hallway and came to a stop in front of a wooden door with a large golden placard that read "Todd Talbot, Bank President." He unlocked the door and ushered the girls inside.

Natural sunlight filled what would have been a very gloomy office. Mr. Talbot had the typical banker's office. A bookcase lined with business books. A wall filled with various diplomas with golden seals. However, there was one standout feature that was unique to his office, there were bowling trophies EVERYWHERE.

If the bank ever went bankrupt, thought Ava, *this guy could make a fortune selling bowling trophies on eBay.*

His ornate desk was incredibly organized—everything was arranged in perfect, straight rows. On the center of his desk sat two very large monitors. The screen on the left was broken up into six little squares that displayed video of the tellers, front door, ATM, and vault in real time. The second monitor displayed a screensaver of his wife and daughter at the beach.

"That's really cool," said Carol as she pointed to the screen with the security videos. "You can see everything that's going on in the bank at once."

Mr. Talbot smiled. "Gotta keep them honest. Come have a look." He motioned to the girls toward the computer screen.

"Okay, let's see here," Mr. Talbot murmured as he entered his computer's password.

A program popped up on the computer screen. Mr. Talbot clicked on a few things and pulled up a separate window. Then a few clicks later, a sharp gray image appeared… the museum!

Ava gasped in delight. She smiled widely at Carol, who looked equally excited.

"Well, it was definitely windy," said Ava, pointing at a piece of string that hung from the ATM's awning—it was whipping back and forth.

"All right, let's see what the camera caught," said Mr. Talbot excitedly. "I believe the news mentioned that the heist happened sometime between 2 a.m. and 5 a.m. So, let's go to two o'clock and fast-forward until we see something. Stop me if I miss anything!"

Ava and Carol nodded—their eyes glued to the screen. Mr. Talbot jumped ahead until the time at the top of the screen read 2:00 in bold white letters. He then began to fast-forward. Everything was calm and quiet…until 3:32 a.m.

"There! There!" said Carol excitedly, pointing at the screen. "It's a delivery truck."

They watched as the truck came to a stop directly in front of the camera, its red taillights illuminating the side of the museum in a transparent sheet of red light. A thick canvas tarp was draped and tied down over the body of the truck.

"Why would they have a tarp over the truck, unless...," said Carol, answering her own question, "...it's hiding something."

Ava nodded in agreement without taking her eyes off the screen.

The driver's side door opened. Ava and Carol expected to see a person climb out of the truck, but instead all they could see was a squat bright fuzzy glowing ball with arms and legs. Seconds later, another glowing ball emerged from the other side of the truck, however it was much taller.

"I'm not really understanding what I'm seeing," said Mr. Talbot.

"Maybe our geography teacher was right. The diamonds were stolen by aliens or Ramesses's spirit," said Ava.

"No," smiled Carol. "It's ingenious. They knew the camera was here. They're wearing some type of reflective material that's making the camera go wonkers."

The two glowing balls paused for a moment at the back of the truck.

"What are they doing?" asked Carol, noticing a bright rectangular light emanating from the shorter blob. "Oh, never mind, I got it. He's talking on the phone."

The phone disappeared back into the glowing blob. The two glowing orbs moved from the back of the truck, and close to the museum. The angle of the ATM camera didn't allow them to see what the two suspects were looking at, but the girls could guess.

"They're looking at the window," whispered Ava.

Suddenly, a ladder dropped into view, stopping about a foot above the ground.

"That's a rope ladder," said Carol, watching as the wind beat it against the building.

"A super-sturdy rope ladder," added Ava.

Mr. Talbot stared intently at the screen. "Girls, you know what this means? This means someone inside the museum is helping them!"

"I kind of figured as much," said Ava.

Everyone was surprised by the two glowing men's agility. They climbed up the precarious ladder with confidence and speed. Ten seconds later, both men completely disappeared from view.

"Obviously someone passed the presidential fitness test. Did you see them climb that ladder?" asked Ava.

"When we catch them," smiled Carol, "the only thing they'll be climbing is the walls of their prison cell."

"Woah," laughed Ava. "That was dark, but much respect for the realism."

"My parents were *way* into *Scared Straight*. I guess it rubbed off on me," said Carol matter-of-factly.

Nothing was happening on the screen, so Mr. Talbot fast-forwarded a few minutes, until the glowing men reappeared.

"They're climbing down!" Mr. Talbot said excitedly.

As soon as they were on the ground, the two glowing bad guys ran to the back of the truck while the ladder slowly ascended out of sight.

"It's kind of sad," said Ava, crossing her arms. "It only took them like ten minutes to steal millions of dollars in diamonds. I can't even brush my hair in ten minutes."

The thieves dashed to the front of the truck and flung open the doors. The digital clock read 3:45 a.m. The taillights flashed on, a puff of smoke erupted from the exhaust pipe and the truck lurched forward. They left in such a hurry, they failed to notice that the bottom corner of the tarp had come loose. As they pulled away, the wind blew, catching it like a sail, causing it to billow up from the side of the truck. It was just a second, but the three observers caught a glimpse of the clue that was about to turn this case around.

"Did you see that?!" said Carol excitedly. "There was writing or some kind of marking on the side of the truck!"

Ava could barely contain herself. They were about to take down a ring of diamond thieves, single-handedly. She thought about the term *single-handed*, but every scenario showed her using both hands to bring down the thieves. *Double-handedly?*

Mr. Talbot clicked a button with his mouse, it allowed him to toggle the video back to the point before the truck sped off. He slowly proceeded frame by frame until they reached the moment where the side of the delivery truck was visible.

"What's it say?" Carol asked, moving around the desk so she could get a better look.

Mr. Talbot froze on frame 10,210. The image was slightly blurred from the exhaust and movement of the truck. There appeared to be letters or numbers and then some sort of squiggly design. Ava edged closer, squinting at the screen, trying to make sense of what she was seeing.

"We need to enchant the picture and make it larger. I can't make out what it says," said Ava, disappointed.

"You mean *enhance* the picture?" said Mr. Talbot, looking up from the image frozen on his screen.

"No. Enchant it, so we could see it better."

Carol's eyes opened wide. "Ava, you're a genius! You mean the Photo Magic Software, right?"

"That's it," Ava snapped. "I just couldn't remember the name of the software."

"Mr. Talbot, is it OK if I commandeer your computer for two minutes? Ava and I use an online software called Hugo's Photo Magic Software in art class. It's an online photo editing software and it should allow me to zoom in and enchant...," she winked at Ava, "...the image. They call editing the image *enchanting*, to go along with the theme of their software."

"Oh," smiled Mr. Talbot. "That makes more sense. But how are you going to get the image from the video?" He pushed himself back from the desk.

"A little something we like to call screen capture," said Ava, smiling and wiggling her eyebrows.

"If you hold down the *Alt* button on your keyboard and then press the *PrtSc* button, it will take a picture of whatever window is selected on your screen," said Carol. "Then all I do is upload that picture right into Hugo's Photo Magic Software."

Mr. Talbot stared at the girls as if they were aliens. "I'm impressed. This isn't hacking, right?" he asked, slightly concerned.

"No!" laughed Carol. "Ava and I only use hacking when we break through the school's firewalls and change our grades."

"Straight A's for life," laughed Ava, high-fiving her friend. Mr. Talbot looked mortified.

"We're just kidding," smiled Carol, seeing Mr. Talbot's expression.

"We get our A's the old-fashioned way. We bribe our teachers," said Ava, playfully nodding.

"Oh, I'm not hearing this," he said, putting his hands to his ears. "Not hearing this."

"We're just playing, Mr. Talbot," said Carol reassuringly. Her fingers then flew across the keyboard. First, she opened the web browser and loaded Hugo's Photo Magic Software. Next, she took a screenshot of the video and saved it to his desktop. She clicked a square that said *Upload*, navigated to the image and uploaded it. Seconds later, it popped into Hugo's Photo Magic Edit screen.

"Okay," Carol said, feeling *in the zone*. "Now I'm going to do what's called sharpening. This will help us see the image more clearly." Carol clicked a menu that read *filters* and selected *sharpen* from the drop-down menu. Not satisfied with the results, she repeated the *sharpen* command once again.

"Whoa," said Mr. Talbot. "Incredible!"

"I'm not done yet," said Carol as she cropped the picture. She then pressed *Zoom*. The result was perfect. They were staring at the number 346, and what appeared to be the bottom edge of a painting… and perhaps a statue.

"Ohhh, 346," whispered everyone together.

"It's either an address or a telephone number," deduced Carol.

"My money is on a telephone number, and the thing above it kind of looks like the bottom of a picture or painting and some sort of sculpture," said Ava.

"It does," nodded Carol in agreement. "What do you think, Mr. Talbot?"

"I wonder if it's part of their logo… but whose?" he said, racking his brain. "It looks very familiar."

A sharp rap on Mr. Talbot's door made everyone jump. He glanced at his watch and shook his head. "I'm sorry, girls. My 1:30 appointment is here," he said, looking disappointed.

"Not a problem at all," said Carol, smiling. "You wouldn't mind if I copied the image of the truck, would you? It won't take but a second."

"Certainly, go right ahead."

"Great!" Carol unsnapped a wristband that doubled as a USB drive. She plugged it into his computer and dragged the image to her drive.

"Gifts from the computer club," said Ava, noticing the concerned look on Mr. Talbot's face. "You realize that you have literally helped us blow this case wide open."

Mr. Talbot's face lit up. "You really think so? It was a lot of fun," he said, smiling broadly. "Promise me you'll let me know how the case is progressing."

"You got it!" smiled Carol as she hopped up from his computer. "Be sure to give my dad a call. Like you said, he needs to get back up on that horse."

"I sure will," Mr. Talbot smiled kindly. He opened his office door. A sharply dressed woman in an immaculate blue business suit stood waiting patiently for him. She smiled and gave a polite wave to Ava and Carol.

She quickly turned her attention back to Mr. Talbot. "Your 1:30 appointment, Mrs. McKinney, is here."

"Thank you, Linda," said Mr. Talbot with a smile. "Please let Mrs. McKinney know I'll be with her in just a moment."

He turned toward the girls as Linda disappeared down the hall. "Ava," he said, reaching out and shaking her hand, "it was a pleasure meeting you, and I'll be sure to watch the ATM video footage for future Hollywood stars like yourself."

He gave Carol a friendly squeeze on her shoulder. "Good luck and be careful!"

"Thank you, Mr. Talbot. I will."

He held the door for the girls as they quickly made their way into the bank lobby.

"Before we leave, I feel like we should pay our respects," Ava gestured to the candy bowl.

"I agree," said Carol. "We'll need energy for the ride home."

Hands filled with candy, and their spirits high, the girls hurried to their bikes. This was the big break they needed!

6
SECRET NINJA CROUCH SLIDE
(DON'T TRY THIS AT HOME)

Sock-footed, Ava slid across her bedroom floor and swiped her laptop off her chest of drawers in one fell swoop. She had once attempted to slide with her no-slip-grip socks and the result had been tragic.

Meanwhile down in the kitchen, Carol was struggling with the sucker wrapper. She eventually gave up, impaled the plastic wrapper with a steak knife and ripped it off. She returned to the table taunting her sucker—*hello, my purple friend, be prepared to meet your demise.*

She was just about to enjoy the fruity flavor when Ava slid across the kitchen, through the door, into the living room. A second later, Ava reappeared, walking nonchalantly with her laptop.

"Nice slide," said Carol approvingly. "Your technique was flawless."

"Thank you," smiled Ava as she placed the laptop on the kitchen table. "They say it's the socks that make the slide. Rubbish! It's pure athleticism and skill." She opened her laptop and typed in her password. An alert popped up reminding her of her piano recital the following Thursday. "Boring...."

"You're so lucky," Carol said. "You get to play the piano—I have to play the bassoon."

"You were the one who raised your hand to play the bassoon in the band. The only one," laughed Ava.

"No," said Carol, sadly shaking her head. "I was raising my hand to go to the restroom. It just happened to be at the same time Mr. Ownby said, 'Bassoon. Any takers?'"

"Ah, I remember the moment. He was so proud of you. And think about it, you're the lead bassoonist!"

"I'm the *only* bassoonist," groaned Carol.

"That makes you the best," said Ava, punching her friend's shoulder.

"Awesome… all my dreams have been fulfilled. I can stop playing the lottery."

"Perfect. That means you are ready to focus on the case."

"If it means you'll stop talking, then yes."

Ava opened her laptop and slid it over to Carol, who navigated to Google Chrome and clicked on Hugo's Photo Magic Software from Ava's favorites. She slipped off her USB bracelet and stuck it into the laptop. Once the program loaded, Carol opened the folder and uploaded the image. The newly enchanted image filled the screen.

"Your talents are limitless," Ava praised. "You never cease to amaze me."

"Flattery will get you nowhere," Carol sighed. "So, looking at the image, there are three components revealed. You may want to get your tiny notebook out for this."

"You're so funny, *not*."

"Ignoring that comment and moving on. The first clue is the number 346, which we've pretty much established is part of a phone number. The next," Carol zoomed in, "is the lower half of a face."

Ava nodded. "It's a woman's mouth and chin. There is something so familiar about that smile… I know I've seen it before."

"It does look familiar," Carol agreed. "The third clue is the statue. It looks like it's part of a bust of someone's head. Perhaps a famous historical figure like Caesar or David."

"David," Ava rolled her eyes. "I hate that statue. He needs a fig leaf or some board shorts," said Ava emphatically.

"Businesses like to use famous icons as their logos or trademarks. Let's see if we can find any telephone numbers that end in 346 and have something in common with the artwork."

Ava tapped her incredibly small pencil against her forehead. "I know that mouth. Don't worry it'll come to me."

"Ah, the infamous forehead tapping. I've done that a few times," smiled Ava's mom as she sauntered into the kitchen. She had her hair pulled back in a loose ponytail and wore midnight blue glasses atop her head. She was holding a bright orange coffee mug that read "Ain't No Hood Like Parenthood."

"Afternoon, Mom," said Ava, deep in thought.

"Good afternoon, Mrs. Clarke," smiled Carol, beaming up at Ava's mom. "I love the glasses!"

"Good afternoon, and thank you, Carol. How's the investigation coming along?" she asked in the middle of a stretch yawn.

"How did you even know we were investigating something?"

"Mom's intuition. My journalistic power of observation. My ability to spot a story from a mile away."

"That's incredible," said Carol.

"Actually, I used these," she said, pointing to her ears. "You two aren't exactly quiet, you know?"

"Ah yes, the formidable parental listening device," whispered Ava. "They've been my nemesis since I was a child."

Mrs. Clarke placed a hand on the table and took a sip of coffee. "Care to share, or is this top secret?"

Carol looked at Ava, afraid to speak first, fearing that she may break some type of friendship trust rule by divulging information. Ava gave her the smallest of nods.

"So," Carol squinched up her face, afraid to continue. "Ava and I have been collecting clues, trying to solve the museum robbery...."

"Before you say anything, Mom, we're just doing our own safe investigation. We're not talking to anyone, we're just looking at clues—call it, *solving-from-afar*."

"Oh," said Ava's mom as she put down her coffee cup. She crossed her arms and turned her attention back to Carol.

Carol wasn't sure if it was an *Oh* as in *Interesting* or an *Oh* as in *You did what? You're grounded for life*. She eyed Ava's mom, trying to sort out her expression as she talked. "And we've made a major breakthrough." Carol looked at Ava, who waved her hand for her to continue. "In a nutshell, we visited the museum and learned that the thieves broke in through the second-story window, and that they had inside help. We also learned that some of the security video had simply vanished."

Ava nodded and took up the story. "Then Carol had the brilliant idea of going to the bank across the street because the ATM camera faces the side of the museum and the window they used to get in."

"That's good detective work," smiled Ava's mom.

"Mr. Talbot let us watch the bank's ATM video. And this is where it gets really interesting," said Ava.

"Gets? This is already fascinating," said Mrs. Clarke, transforming from mom to journalist. "What did the video show?"

"A delivery truck pulled up to the museum in the middle of the night," answered Ava. "The bad guys wore some kind of reflective clothing that made them look like aliens."

"Interesting," said Mrs. Clarke. "Thieves are using modified glasses that reflect light. It pretty much blinds the camera."

"They tried to be sneaky by covering the side of the truck with a tarp, but the wind was blowing like crazy. It lifted the tarp and we saw the number 346 and we're guessing this is some type of logo." Ava pointed to the picture on the screen. "There's the bottom half of a woman's face and a statue."

Mrs. Clarke leaned in and stared at the screen. "Ah, I see you only have the bottom of the nose and the lips of the woman." Ava's mom began to smile, just like the woman in the painting. "You know who that smile belongs to, right? It's a very famous painting…. May I?" she asked, pointing to the laptop.

"Sure, Mom, go for it."

Mrs. Clarke opened a new tab in the browser. Her fingers quickly raced across the keyboard. She smiled and turned the laptop around to show the girls.

"Ugh!" said Carol, smacking her forehead. "Of course! *Mona Lisa*, painted by Leonardo da Vinci!"

"Mom, you're a genius. Thank you!" said Ava proudly.

"You girls would have figured it out. May I see the image of the van one more time?"

"It's still open," said Ava as she turned the laptop back toward her mom. "Carol thinks that the statue or sculpture is Caesar."

Ava's mom stared at the image and nodded. "That's a great guess. You can see the chin and the neck... and the armor with the fringes on the shoulders. Again, this is a very famous sculpture. I think Carol's right."

"Now we just need to figure out who has a logo with Mona Lisa and Caesar, and 346 as the last three digits of their phone number!" said Carol excitedly.

"Oh, I forgot to ask. How did you know the thieves robbed the museum through a window?"

"We watched them," said Carol. "Someone from inside the museum threw a rope ladder down and they climbed up it. So we know that at least three people are involved."

The thought of the criminals seemed to jar something loose in Ava's mom. "Girls," she said softly, in a tone that every child recognizes as *I'm proud of you, but now it's time to back off.* "I don't mind if you work on clues here or someplace safe, like the library... but these thieves can be dangerous, and I don't want anything to happen to you."

Ava felt like her mother had put training wheels on her ten-speed. *This is our first real case and Mom is already putting on the brakes.* "Mom, we're so close. We'll be super careful," said Ava, her voice filled with disappointment. "You always said I had great instincts—that I was just like you when you were a kid. I *know* how to keep myself out of danger. And…," Ava said, gesturing toward Carol, "…she plays the *bassoon*! Tell me, in all your life as an investigative journalist, have you *ever* heard of a bassoonist getting in trouble *or* putting their life in danger?" Ava gave her mother an *I rest my case* look.

"And again… she casts shade on me…," whispered Carol. She made a mental note to adorn Ava's locker, her notebooks, her bike, her forehead with stickers that read, "Bassoon Life."

Ava's mom stared at her daughter for what felt like an eternity. "I will let you continue your investigation—"

"Thank you! Thank you!" Ava interrupted, jumping up to hug her mom.

"Wait," she said, putting a hand on each of Ava's shoulders, staring into her eyes. "If I even get a *hint* that you girls are doing anything even *remotely* dangerous, your investigation stops." She looked from Ava to Carol and back to Ava. "Is that understood?" she asked seriously.

"Yes, ma'am," they answered quietly.

"Okay," smiled Mrs. Clarke. "Get to work— you've got a case to solve. And I've got an article to write about an eccentric rich man in Ireland. Ironically, they think that this guy may be connected to the millions of dollars' worth of paintings stolen from the Isabella Stewart Gardner Museum."

"That's incredible, Mom. So, they've tracked the paintings to Ireland?"

"How did the pictures get all the way to Ireland?" asked Carol.

"They have secret crime rings that are experts at moving stolen goods out of the country. Private dealers pay thieves millions of dollars to steal and sneak them out of the U.S."

"So, someone like the rich guy in Ireland could do the same thing with the diamonds that were stolen from the museum, right?"

"Yes. Matter of fact, the same mysterious millionaire in Ireland just put a pre-bid on Chopin's piano and the original hand-scored version of *Prelude No. 4* at a private auction. Together, they are worth well over $15 million. I wasn't supposed to know this," she said, giving a mischievous smile, "but I do have a secret, inside source."

"Secret? By secret source you mean Detective Edwards," said Ava matter-of-factly.

Her mother blushed for just a moment, then she quickly regained her composure. "Yes, Blake does help me on occasion."

Carol looked from Ava to Mrs. Clarke, confused.

"My mom and her *secret source* went to middle school and high school together," Ava explained. "They were king and queen of the senior prom. Dad was the kid who presented their crowns. He said tears were streaming down Mom's face when their eyes met."

"Wow, so romantic!" exclaimed Carol.

"I was in pain…," explained Mrs. Clarke. "He poked me in the eye when he put the crown on my head."

"Hey, he said he stole your heart like a thief in the night," said Ava, "and I believe him."

"The only thing he stole like a thief in the night was that powder blue tux and white loafers," Mrs. Clarke said. "Somewhere, there's a naked 1980s mannequin missing a leisure suit."

"Oh my God," Carol snorted, picturing Ava's dad in a powder blue tuxedo.

"Mom, if prom king knows who this guy is, why doesn't he work with the police in Ireland? Can't they just search his house for the missing paintings? He probably has tons of famous stolen stuff!"

"It would be great if it were that easy," her mom replied. "No one is quite sure who he is. Everything is purchased through a series of brokers—and he pays them very well. Supposedly, one broker threatened to reveal his identity… he was never seen again."

"Whoa," whistled Ava, "these guys are serious. I wouldn't want to be called a broker if I worked with priceless art. I think I would rather be called a fixer."

Ava's mother shook her head. "A broker is a person that's like a professional shopper. Rich people use experts like these to make purchases for them so they can buy things anonymously. The broker is usually paid a percentage of the sale."

"They don't only work with shady deals though. My dad uses a stockbroker and real estate brokers."

"Correct," said Mrs. Clarke. "There are good and bad brokers, just like there are good and bad businesspeople. As you learn more about the criminal world, you'll learn that there are very sophisticated crime rings that run just like a business. It's why it's called organized crime."

"Wait. Mrs. Clarke, is your article going to discuss this mysterious guy's identity? I'm only asking because that sounds very dangerous. Like you said, the last guy disappeared."

Ava's smile literally melted from her face. "Mom, you're not really gonna try to find out who this guy is, are you?"

"Yes, I am going to try to find out who he is. But no, I'm not going to try to expose him," Mrs. Clarke smiled reassuringly. "We'd have to go into witness protection, and I kind of like our neighborhood and friends."

Ava didn't look one hundred percent convinced. She didn't like the thought of anything bad happening to her mom. She got up and gave her a big hug. "Be careful, please. You're the only mom I've got."

Mrs. Clarke hugged Ava tightly. "Don't you worry. I'll be careful." She grabbed her coffee from the table, and walked across the kitchen, stopping in the doorway. "Let me know if you need me."

"We will, Mom, thanks again." Ava turned back to Carol as her mom left the kitchen, a determined look on her face. "If this guy is the same guy behind this robbery, he is going to rue the day he was born."

"*Rue*," Carol said, smiling at her friend. "Ingenious."

7
HOW DO YOU SOLVE
A PROBLEM LIKE A LOGO?

Master bassoonist Klaus Thunemann's greatest hits belted from the tiny speaker in Carol's phone. He was just into the kicker of the woeful "JC Bach Concerto" when Ava screamed, "Uncle!"

"What? I particularly enjoy this piece. It's devilishly difficult, don't you think?" smirked Carol innocently. "Imagine the finger placement, so complex!"

"I'm imagining some finger placement right now, and they're around your neck."

"You're missing the point. Classical music is supposed to be calming. Relax your shoulders and let it fill your soul."

"You're about to feel the sole of my foot! Seriously, enough with the woodwinds."

"Fine," sighed Carol, "but I was making tremendous progress."

"Really?" said Ava skeptically.

"Yes, I've made a list of the businesses that would most likely have a logo composed of those historical elements. Would you like to hear my list?"

"Of course. Amaze me."

"Art stores, schools, home and business decorating stores and museums."

"Eh, that's pretty good. I would think our best bet would be an art store. The only trucks I've ever seen at our school were mail trucks, FedEx—"

"Or those food trucks for the cafeteria," added Carol.

"Or... some type of business that caters to museums, maybe some type of renovation business?"

Ava nodded. "I'm going to guess that the business would have to be somewhat local. I can't imagine them driving a truck around in the middle of the night with a tarp on it. Nothing says suspicious like driving your truck around wrapped up like a burrito."

"Oh my God," laughed Carol. "Actually, I could go for a burrito right now. I'm starving."

"Me too," said Ava.

"Me three," came a voice from the living room.

"That woman's hearing scares me.... I truly believe she was a bat in her previous life."

"I heard that!" yelled Ava's mother.

"See?" said Ava, making an *I told you so* face. "Alrighty," she said, turning her attention back to her laptop. "If I draw a twenty-mile circle with the museum being in the center, it includes Livingston, Lexington, Concord and Middleville."

"I guess we should start with Livingston. I can't imagine there will be many art stores," said Carol.

"Yep," said Ava, "I'm on it."

Luckily, Livingston was a small town of twelve thousand people. Ava's search brought up two art stores and an outdoor faux statue garden center. Nothing says *sophisticated* like poorly made Romanesque statues with an accompanying spotlight for your front yard.

Livingston was a complete bust (no pun intended). The number 346 didn't show up in any of the stores' telephone numbers or street addresses. Thirty minutes later, the girls had exhausted all their searches. Not being easily defeated, they expanded their search out another twenty miles, but after another exhaustive search, nothing matched the elusive number.

"I don't get it," said Carol disappointedly. "We searched for phone numbers, for addresses. Who else would have a logo with the painting of Mona Lisa or a Caesar on their truck?"

"A pizza delivery truck?" offered Ava.

Carol brought the picture back up on the computer. "I don't feel like Mona's hungry. I think she's laughing at us. Look at that pretentious smile."

"Oh, you two are on a first-name basis? Suddenly, I feel like the awkward third wheel."

"Me and Mona are besties," laughed Carol. "You know, I'm surprised no one ever stole the *Mona Lisa*. The painting is actually super small, less than two feet wide."

"Really? I always thought the painting was giant. Smuggling a famous painting out of the country seems so simple. You could put it in a FedEx tube and ship it to your buyer. It's not likely they examine every one of those tubes."

"Ava...," whispered Carol, her eyes growing wide. "You're a genius."

"Of course I am," said Ava, her face filling with pride. "Now tell me why."

"Remember when your mom was talking about the private auction, and smuggling stuff out of the country?"

"Yes...."

"Do a search on private auction companies?" asked Carol excitedly.

"Sure." She typed in the words *private auction company* and pressed *Enter*.

Carol scooched her chair against Ava's so she could see the search results. Livingston returned zero results. However, Google revealed a rectangular map, showing two auction companies in the surrounding towns—one in Concord, the other in Middleville.

Only two of the companies listed a website, but the thing that caught their eyes was the Middleville listing. It just happened to have a telephone number ending in 346.

Ava's heart leapt in her chest. "Bingo—346," she whispered.

"That's got to be it!" exclaimed Carol excitedly.

Ava clicked on the link, and seconds later, they were staring at the ornately written words "Prestige Fine Arts Auction Company," and beneath the company name was a very familiar logo of the Mona Lisa and Julius Caesar.

"We found it!" whispered Ava.

"Ava, if my hunch is right, and my hunchiness meter is feeling extremely hunchy, we've just found out who stole the diamonds."

"Your hunchiness is strong, my friend," Ava said. "So you think they're gonna try to sell the diamonds at a private auction? Seems gutsy… and dumb."

"I don't think they would be dumb enough to risk auctioning them. Especially since they were just stolen. I think they have something more creative in mind."

"Similar to my FedEx idea?"

"Very similar," nodded Carol, "but it's not so simple. FedEx takes x-rays of all their packages, so it's too big a risk. Plus, what if the diamonds got lost or stolen by an unscrupulous employee?"

"And we already said that you can't hide them on your person or in your luggage."

"Right," agreed Carol, "because you have to go through Customs. The x-ray machine would definitely spot those. But, and this is a big but—"

Ava snorted. "Sorry, you have to admit that's funny."

Carol sighed and continued, "What if the theft is tied to the billionaire your mom is researching? I mean, think about it. It's the perfect plan. Steal the diamonds, hide them in a priceless antique and then ship them out of the country, hidden inside."

"It's an amazing theory," said Ava. "How do we find out which auction he is bidding on? If you look, they have half a dozen auctions, and then two private auctions."

"Right there," said Carol, jabbing her index finger at the screen. "Click the *Scheduled Auctions* link." The girls waited for the page to load. "Scroll down a little. Stop!" Carol exclaimed. "No! They only list the dates for the public auctions."

"Oh yeah, it says private auctions by invitation only."

"It makes sense. Private auctions wouldn't be very private if the public could see all the details. My guess is they have a select group of people that they work with to ensure secrecy."

"What about this?" asked Ava. "It says auction manifest."

"Manifest? That's usually a list of items. You know, like a ship would have a manifest of what's onboard."

Ava tapped the touchpad on her laptop. A PDF began to open, but then a password window appeared over it. "Never mind, it's password protected," moaned Ava.

"Let me see that," said Carol. She spun the laptop around. "Sorry for commandeering your laptop. Wow," she said staring at the screen, "that's some pretty weak protection."

"Maybe, we could call them and get some information about the auctions," offered Ava.

"Probably not. I mean, they would probably tell you about the public auctions but… I have a better idea," said Carol, a gleam in her eyes.

"You're not going to—"

"Hack them? No. No. No," Carol chuckled. "I'm just going to test how secure their webpage is. Later, if they're not involved in criminal activity, we'll let them know how they can improve their web security. I'm actually doing them a favor."

"And my mom thinks *I'm* the one she has to keep an eye on."

"It's always the quiet ones," snickered Carol. She quickly connected to her home computer and shared the screen. She opened a terminal window and began typing. "I have a text document that has millions of words on it, starting with the letter A. I'll run a program that will test every word on my list to see if it's the same as their password."

"What if it's not on your list?" asked Ava.

"Then we'll try something else." Carol pressed the start button. Instantly, the screen filled with the auction company's URL address and words from

Carol's text list. "This could take a couple hours. They most likely have an alphanumeric password."

"I'm guessing that means a combination of letters and numbers."

"You got it. Those are the hardest to—never mind," Carol shook her head in disbelief. "We're in. Their password is literally P@55w0rd."

Carol clicked *OK*, and the password window disappeared. A second later, an official-looking PDF document opened. The header read "Prestige Fine Arts Auction Company." Beneath the header was "Lot 1422."

"Ava," said Carol, stunned. "We've got him!"

"What do you mean we've got him?" asked Ava, confused.

"Look at what the first item on the manifest is: Chopin's Camille Pleyel piano!" Carol's eyes dropped down to the next item on the auction list: autographed *Prelude Number Four*. "That's the same piano your mom was telling us about!"

"Yeah, that's *way* too much of a coincidence. Does it say when the auction is going to take place?"

"No, it says they will receive an email with a link to the private bidding portal twenty-four hours before the auction."

"Are you able to get into their emails?" asked Ava.

"No, that requires access to their server. All I did was access their website. Accessing their email client is a whole different ballgame."

"So what do we do? The auction could be tomorrow and then we'll be too late." Carol fell back into her seat and closed her eyes, deep in thought. "We've got to find out where they're going to hide the diamonds and stop them!"

"Everything okay in here?" asked Ava's mom, poking her head through the doorway, a twinge of concern on her face.

Carol jumped at Mrs. Clarke's voice, almost flipping the chair over backward.

"I'm sorry, Carol. I didn't mean to startle you," laughed Ava's mom.

"It's okay," said Carol, recovering. "I was just deep in thought."

"You guys have been at this for quite some time. How about some dinner? Perhaps Burrito Gordito?"

"*Burrito Gordito es mi favorito*!" exclaimed Ava. "I've been sitting so long I can no longer feel my legs. My buttocks are tingling."

Ava's mom shook her head and sighed. "Carol, would you like to come to dinner with us? Or perhaps you'd rather escape while you still can?"

"That sounds great, Mrs. Clarke. Thank you."

"So, you're picking the *escape while you can* choice?" laughed Ava's mom.

"Yep!" smiled Carol.

Ava placed her hand dramatically over her heart. "It's shattered. Broken into tiny, tiny pieces," she whispered. She closed her eyes and then opened one, just a smidge, so she could see Carol's reaction.

"Fine," said Carol, shaking her head. "I'll come to dinner with you."

"Really? I could have cared less," said Ava with a shrug. "Youth today, so easily manipulated."

8
OPERATION ANACONDA

Location: Burrito Gordito, Mexican restaurant, 5:45 p.m.

"There I was, in the belly of a giant metal anaconda, surrounded by microscopic bacterial organisms!" Ava's dad paused to take a bite of his beef burrito.

"Dad, weren't you in the ventilation system at an aquarium?"

"Don't knock my dramatic flair," smiled her dad. "Look, you don't make it on the Discovery Channel by being boring. You could help, you know, by adding some dramatic music."

"That would be Carol. She could mesmerize any audience with her haunting woodwind overtures," said Ava, pointing her burrito at her friend.

"Oh my God, Ava, let your dad finish! I for one am on the edge of my seat, Mr. Clarke."

"More like the edge of insanity…," muttered Ava.

Ava turned to her dad. "You're a marine biologist…. Aren't you supposed to be researching things involving um, I don't know, water?"

"If you'd let me finish my story, everything will make sense!" exclaimed Mr. Clarke.

"Let your father have his moment," said Ava's mother, patting her hand.

"He's gonna get exasperated, isn't he? I hate it when he gets exasperated. Last Christmas, it was that cheerful story he told about Legionnaires disease that made the holiday so much lovelier."

"I know," her mother smiled. "I'm sure this one ends on a much happier note... right, Charles?" She gave him that special look that meant *happy ending or we're having meatloaf the rest of the week.*

"Yes, of course, dear. I do hope you know that you've completely destroyed the momentum of my story.... Now, where was I?"

"In the belly of the avocado...," muttered Ava.

"Anaconda! Ah, yes! My headlamp began to flicker, sweat poured down my face, and then I realized my egregious mistake. I had left the Q-tip swabs in my pocket. Not to be deterred, and thanks to my years of yoga—using the *soaring eagle tilts its wings* technique, I maneuvered in such a way that I was able to retrieve the swabs from my pocket!"

"Way to go, Mr. Clarke!" beamed Carol.

"Thank you, Carol," said Mr. Clarke, nodding appreciatively. "I reached out slowly, my hands shaking. What crazed organism inhabited this metallic serpent?"

"It's a question we are all asking ourselves," winked Ava.

"With expert precision, I collected the deadly samples and began crawling backward! Just in time too, because the huge exhaust fan at the end of the ventilation system kicked in. A quick side note, I was having a brilliant hair day until then….”

“So, I’m glad you survived, Dad. Your story is truly epic, and I believe the table next to us was enthralled too.”

Ava’s dad looked at the table beside them. An Indian family rewarded him with a smattering of applause.

“Thank you,” he said graciously, acknowledging their gratitude. “So, I know you are all wondering what evil pathogen I discovered.”

“Yes,” whispered Carol.

“Yes,” chorused the Indian family, leaning forward in their seats.

“It turned out to be…,” he paused dramatically, “the nefariously evil, Stachybotrys!”

“Ohhh,” exclaimed the Indian woman in a high-pitched voice. She dropped her fork to her plate with a clatter as her husband patted her hand.

“Horrible,” the man whispered.

Ava’s father nodded. “Yes, indeed.”

“I’m sorry, stackybots what?” asked Ava.

“Black mold. The staff at the aquarium kept getting sick with crazy respiratory problems, and no one could figure out why. I had a hunch that it could be the air they were breathing in. Sure enough, their ventilation system was filled with it. I don’t like to brag—modesty and my doctoral ethics prevents me from doing so—but I'm pretty sure I saved their lives."

Another smattering of applause erupted from the Indian family.

Mr. Clarke accepted their platitudes graciously by nodding and mouthing *thank you.*

"Great job, Dad," said Ava, beaming proudly. "A real-world example of biology in action!"

"Great story, Mr. Clarke," smiled Carol. "Excuse me, I'll be right back." She pushed her chair from the table and headed toward the restroom.

"Great. See, Dad? Your story gave her indigestion."

"That's ludicrous," said Mr. Clarke, brushing away Ava's comment. "Carol's very astute and simply appreciates *quality* storytelling."

Ava's mind drifted away from the dinner table as her parents settled into a conversation about work and current events. She felt guilty not sharing everything that she and Carol had discovered with her parents, but they were so close to solving the mystery. Ava jumped as her phone vibrated against her leg.

Her eyes flew up to her parents, expecting them to ask her why she jumped, but they were deep into their conversation and hadn't noticed.

Ava needed to get her phone out without being seen. There was one rule that her parents enforced, NO PHONES AT THE TABLE!

She tried covering her phone with the black cloth napkin, but she couldn't see the message. She looked around, and then her eyes narrowed. "Ma'am," she called out to the waitress who was wiping down a table across from her. "May I have a dessert menu?"

The waitress smiled. "Just one?"

Her parents looked up, trying to catch up to Ava's conversation. "Good point. You may want to bring three. My parents love coffee with their ice cream."

"Thank you, Ava, that was really thoughtful," smiled her mom.

"You're welcome," Ava returned the smile.

The waitress returned with the menus. Ava's mom thanked her, and soon, everyone's attention was turned to perusing the delicious desserts. As her parents focused on a sugary delicacy, Ava stealthily slid her phone out of her pocket. She clicked on the text message. Carol had sent a picture of the top of a large industrial building, and under it were the words "Prestige Fine Arts Auction Company."

Ava stared at the picture of the top of the building and texted back, "How far away is that bathroom?"

A moment later, Ava's phone buzzed again. "Your dad gave me the idea. It's our way into the building. Their ventilation system."

"Are you sending me all of this from a bathroom stall?"

"Yes. I was sitting here, thinking."

"You want us to break into the prestige auction house? And my mom thinks you are the responsible one."

"Do you want to stop the thieves?"

"Of course, but can we just talk about this when we get back to my house…"

"It's the only way, Aves. We'll call it, *Operation Anaconda!*" Carol texted back.

Ava could hear Carol's voice in her head, bubbling over with excitement. "Are you returning to the table anytime soon, or should I have a care package sent to the restroom?"

"Care package sounds great, stall number three."

9
CAROL GETS A CHANCE TO VENT

Carol stared out the car window, willing Ava's dad to drive more quickly. *I should have insisted on him getting the double espresso.* It was already 7:15 p.m. and getting dark outside. In order for her master plan to succeed, they needed to get to the auction house fast, without Ava's parents finding out.

"You girls are mighty quiet. Everything okay back there?" Ava's mom turned toward the girls, leaning between the front seats.

"Yes. I'm in the midst of a food coma," Ava moaned. "I think the double-layer chocolate fudge cake with two scoops of vanilla ice cream did me in. I may find the closest lake and beach myself on the shore."

"You should have split it with Carol like your dad and I did. The cinnamon apple pie was perfect for two people."

"I believe that splitting a dessert in Massachusetts is breaking some sort of town ordinance," Ava replied.

"Definitely against the law," Carol agreed. "It's under the Dessert Sharing Act of 1812. I believe it reads, 'Desserts are not to be shared, anyway, anyhow.'"

"I believe it was amended in 1813 by the Romantic Couples Act," laughed Mrs. Clarke. "I believe it now reads, 'Sharing is caring.'"

"Good one, Mrs. Clarke," Carol grinned.

"Ugh," Ava leaned her forehead against the cool glass of the car window.

"Tonight's a great telescope night," said Ava's dad as they pulled into their driveway. Carol looked up through the moonroof. Even with the front porch light and spotlights illuminating the entire front of the house, they could clearly see the stars.

Ava smiled. "Dad, you're right." She turned to Carol. "We could set up the tent and the telescope. We could tell ghost stories."

Carol caught on to Ava's ruse immediately. "I love that idea. We haven't moon and planet watched in forever!"

"Is it okay if we set up the tent tonight in the backyard?" Ava asked. "We haven't camped out for like months, and it's gonna be cold soon."

"Fine with me," said her dad. "You know me, I never get in the way of you exploring nature… unless you were climbing into an active volcano. That's where I draw the line."

"I lava you, Dad," smiled Ava.

"I lava you, too," he said, erupting with laughter.

~~o~o~o~~

Ava and Carol made a big show of being excited about setting up the tent. They brought out a star guide and a notebook so they could do some sketching. Ava's mom made delicious popcorn cooked in olive oil and sea salt, making the entire house smell edible.

Ava put the popcorn in a freezer bag to keep it fresh and grabbed four juice boxes. Her parents had retired to the living room to watch *You've Got Mail* for the fiftieth time.

"Good night, Mom. Good night, Dad," said Ava as she leaned over and gave each of her parents a hug. "I have my phone, so I'll text you around 3 a.m. if I get lonely."

"Oh wait," said her father as he jumped up from the sofa. He opened the closet and pulled out the largest flashlight Ava had ever seen. "This is the Thor 2000." He cradled it in his arms. "Their motto is 'Put the Hammer Down on Darkness.' I'm not really sure what that means, but this flashlight packs twelve thousand lumens. It will literally turn night to day."

"Thank you, Dad," said Ava as she looked at the huge, clunky flashlight.

"Wield her with care," her father warned. He dropped the flashlight with a *thunk* into Ava's arms.

"Okay, Dad, thank you. I may need Carol to help me carry it back to the tent."

"It's got some weight to it," Mr. Clarke agreed.

"Oh, look, here on the side, says it may be used as a boat anchor."

"Really? Oh, funny, you're messing with me." He leaned in and gave Ava a hug. "Have fun tonight. We'll leave one of the windows unlocked for you," he teased.

"Make sure it's on the second floor. I love a good challenge."

"Will do," laughed Mr. Clarke as he turned back toward the living room. "Love you," he called over his shoulder.

"Love you too, Dad."

Ava hurried over to help Carol who was busy setting up the telescope. "Smart plan, smuggling out the laptop with the sleeping bag," she said.

"Thanks," said Ava. "My parents are busy watching a romantic movie. They'll most likely fall asleep right after that. What's the plan?"

Carol motioned for Ava to follow her into the tent. "Can I use your laptop?" she asked.

"Sure. My laptop, your laptop."

"Thanks," said Carol, flipping open the lid and firing up Google. "Your dad's story about the ventilation system made me realize we could do the same thing to get into the auction house. But I need to check a few things to make sure it will work." Carol logged into Middleville's Building Department system.

"Let me guess, you're searching to see if a teenager can fit into a ventilation shaft," said Ava.

"Close," nodded Carol.

"Really? Because I was just—" Carol turned the laptop so Ava could see the screen. "Contractors have to file their blueprints with the Building Department, and once they do, they become public record," she explained. "This will tell me everything I need to know about the building."

"How the heck do you know that?" inquired Ava, impressed.

"What does my dad do?" asked Carol as she typed in the address of Prestige Fine Arts Auction Company.

"He designs houses and buildings… your dad's an architect."

"So, I am logging in as my dad into the Building Department to find the blueprints for the auction company."

"You're so smart. How does your brain even fit inside that misshapen head?"

"I'll explain density and mass to you later," winked Carol. "I found the blueprint. There are three different entries from the roof." Carol traced her finger along the drawing of the rooftop. "One leads to what looks like a series of offices, the second to restrooms, and the third," she paused to take a closer look, "leads to a small, reinforced room with a massive cement slab. And that only means one thing."

"They have a tiger?" inquired Ava.

"No, you nut, it means they have a safe. They put huge cement slabs down and then attach the safe to them. I betcha a gazillion dollars that's where they are hiding the diamonds."

"You think that they would actually keep the diamonds there?"

"Where else would they hide them?"

"I don't know, a super-secret warehouse somewhere."

"Look, we're dealing with corrupt businessmen. We've already made several important connections. The truck at the scene of the crime. The man your mother is doing the story on and the fact that he is involved in an auction."

"Okay, let's say they have the diamonds. Why not call the police and tell them, we think the diamonds are in that safe?"

"Do you honestly think the police are going to listen to us? Plus, they'll have to get a search warrant. There're just too many ways things could go wrong."

"I always thought I was the one that would get us grounded for life."

"We're not going to get caught. I simply need to get into the ventilation system, get into a computer, grab the information that I need, and then we're out of there."

"That easy, huh?" Ava said, looking doubtful.

"I've been crawling around construction sites my entire life. I've got this!"

Ava was quiet for a moment. She looked at the blueprint again. "You said that narrow rectangular thing is the ventilation system?"

Carol nodded. "Mm-hmm."

"How big is it?"

Carol scanned the blueprint. "Twenty-eight inches by twenty-two inches and it slants on about a forty-five-degree angle. So," she said, standing and creating a box with her arms and hands, "about this big."

"Keep holding that imaginary box. I want to see something," said Ava. She ducked under Carol's arms, then stood up inside the virtual rectangle. "That's a tight fit," said Ava, worriedly.

"Look, it's not going to be a problem," said Carol. "I've helped my dad on tons of projects. Leave the ventilation exploration to me."

Ava wasn't about to put up an argument on that one. "The building is two stories. How do you propose we get to the roof?" Ava asked.

"I haven't figured that one out yet. They have a fire escape on the second floor on each side of the building. We just need to be able to get to it, and it's about twelve feet off the ground."

"We also have to get there," said Ava, "and it's like six miles away."

Carol sat and thought. "Rope?" she suddenly blurted out. "We throw it up to the fire escape and climb up it."

"Perfect," said Ava, "I'll just run inside and get my grappling hook. Oh, wait a minute, my grandmother borrowed it."

"What about a ladder?" suggested Carol.

"Could work but would be really suspicious-looking and incredibly hard to carry on two bikes."

"Wait a second," said Carol. "You're going to hate the idea, but it will work."

"Well then, by all means, please share," laughed Ava.

"My dad showed me how to make a makeshift ladder. The only drawback is you and I are going to have to ride six miles with a board that is ten feet long and weighs about thirty pounds."

"Enlighten me about this board you speak of," Ava said, narrowing her eyes.

"I'll do better than that, I'll show you," Carol smiled.

"Sounds like an adventure," smiled Ava excitedly. "I have a great idea—be right back." She snuck quietly into her house, being careful not to make a sound. While tiptoeing upstairs, she grabbed her backpack, her GoPro and head-strap. She paused as she left her room while whispering, "I love you, Mom. I love you, Dad." She silently crept down the stairs and out the door.

"My great idea," said Ava as she pulled the GoPro from her backpack.

"Oh, that is an awesome idea! Okay, we need to get a few things from my dad's workshop. Come on."

They then ran through the darkness down the street to Carol's house. All the lights were off except for the front porch and two large spotlights that illuminated the front of her dad's giant two-car garage. From somewhere down the street, a deep, throaty *woof, woof* echoed through the night.

The girls crept cautiously down the sidewalk. Carol motioned Ava to follow her as she opened the side door to the building. Carol flicked on her flashlight app, illuminating the interior of her father's workshop. The back of the building was filled with power tools, a giant drill press, a table saw, and lots of lumber. Carol searched through the stacks until she found the board she was looking for.

"Here," she said, lifting the ten-foot-long board. "This will be the base of our ladder."

They laid the board out in the yard beside the garage. Carol looked in her dad's scrap pile filled with small pieces of cut wood. She packed her backpack with half a dozen pieces. Then, she grabbed two rolls of duct tape, a pair of pliers, an adjustable wrench, a flathead screwdriver, a Phillips-head screwdriver, and a coil of rope.

"Geez," whispered Ava, "are you starting your own Home Depot?"

"Trust me," said Carol thoughtfully. "We'll need this stuff."

Ava watched as Carol took the blocks of wood that she had gathered from the scrap pile and duct-taped them one by one onto the ten-foot board. When she was done, she had five pieces of board placed about a foot apart down the length of the board.

At the top, she attached a board horizontally, making the final addition look like a very tall T. She stepped back and admired her work. "This is how we're going to get to the top of the auction building."

"Okay," said Ava. "Care to explain?"

"Yep, it's a makeshift ladder. You lean this against the building, and the T at the top keeps it from wiggling back and forth. The small boards I taped on act as steps."

"Big brain, you're brilliant," said Ava. "I'm impressed!"

"Thanks," laughed Carol. "The other tools are just in case I need them in the ventilation system. All right," said Carol as she checked her phone. "It's 10:07 p.m., and we have an appointment with a ventilation shaft!"

Ava and Carol quickly checked to make sure they had everything they needed, grabbed the makeshift ladder, and silently raced back to Ava's house to grab their bikes. Operation Anaconda was officially launched!

10
CHOPIN'S LAST CONCERTO

Carrying a ten-foot ladder by bike for six miles was no easy task, but the girls made good time. Middleville was slightly larger than Livingston, but thankfully, not many people were out during this time of night.

A cool evening breeze was blowing as the girls pulled up to a small park, directly across the street from Prestige Fine Arts Auction Company.

"We made it," whispered Ava, keeping her voice low.

They quickly checked their surroundings and then hid their bikes, laying them down in a small clump of trees. They broke off some low-hanging branches to cover their bikes as an extra precaution. The last thing they needed was to have their bikes stolen in the middle of their mission.

Prestige Fine Arts Auction Company seemed out of place in Middleville—a small, historic town founded in 1786. Amongst houses of stone and red brick stood a modern geometric spectacle. The walls were made of perfectly polished gray stone, with long, narrow, rectangular windows across the top. The roof jutted out like slices of bread in all different angles. Bright orange light emanated from within, illuminating the building like a huge candle. Outside, the parking lot looked like a virtual forest of perfectly pruned ficus trees bathed in a white glow, illuminated by dozens of security spotlights.

"Okay," said Carol as she looked at the auction building. "According to the blueprints, there is a fire escape on each side of the building."

"That building is huge," said Ava. "And it's super well lit… and we didn't have time to do reconnaissance, so we have no idea what type of security they have."

"Well," said Carol, watching as two cars drove past, "let's get the ladder across the street and hide by those trees." She pointed to the edge of the auction house's parking lot. "It's the darkest area, and we can watch for a few minutes and see if we see anyone."

"Okay," Ava nodded and checked out the road that separated them from the parking lot. "All clear." They grabbed the ladder, bolted across the road, and dropped down behind a cluster of bushes and trees, deep in the shadows.

"Okay," said Carol. "We'll watch for ten minutes. Hopefully, they're—"

"In a golf cart, heading this way," whispered Ava urgently.

The girls dropped flat to the ground as two men in black shirts with black hats that read "Security" passed within ten feet of them. A spotlight, mounted to the top of the golf cart, swept back and forth, creating a wide swath of light in front of them.

Luckily, the men were more interested in their conversation than what was going on around them. Ava and Carol slowly raised their heads above the bushes and watched the golf cart move away from them to the side of the building.

One of the guards got out and shone his light behind a huge dumpster, and then up the fire escape. Satisfied, he got back on the cart with his partner. They drove the length of the building—red brake lights flashing—and then disappeared around the back.

"Okay," said Ava quietly. "That answers the security question."

"I wonder how long it takes them to make their loop."

"Good question. We better time them, just to make sure. I'd hate to say that I got chased down by security guards in a golf cart."

"True," said Carol. "Almost as bad as a Segway cop at the mall." She looked down at her watch. "They've been gone one minute so far."

"Get down!" whispered Ava urgently, yanking Carol's shoulder. They just missed being lit up like Christmas trees as a black Mercedes pulled into the parking lot. They watched as the car made its way to the main entrance of the building.

The front door of the building swung open, and a man briskly walked out to the car. Two men in dark suits emerged from the vehicle. The man shook the driver's hand and then shook the other man's hand as they came together in a small huddle. The man from the auction house gestured to the entranceway and escorted them inside.

"Geez, that was close. That's another thing we'll have to be aware of," whispered Carol. "Surprise guests!"

Three minutes later, the girls could see the lights coming from the golf cart. The security guards weren't as unobservant as the girls had thought. They made a beeline across the parking lot to inspect the new vehicle. They parked their golf cart behind the Mercedes so it couldn't back away. One of the guards touched his ear and spoke.

"I bet he's checking on the car," whispered Carol.

Ava nodded. "They don't mess around."

"Especially when you're protecting millions of dollars of inventory."

The security guard nodded, said something to his partner, and they resumed their loop. Once again, the girls dropped silently to the ground. The golf cart came within twenty feet of the girls. It was so close, they could hear the guards talking about the upcoming Patriots game.

"All right, Aves," said Carol nervously. "As soon as those taillights disappear around the corner, we run to that stairwell. We'll have about three and a half minutes—that's it."

Just as before, the golf cart came to a stop in front of the fire escape. This time the other guard jumped out, first shining his light behind the dumpster and then checking out the fire escape. Seconds later, the taillights flickered, disappearing around the corner of the building.

"Okay," said Carol, electricity pumping through her body, "we're gonna have to be fast and furious. Let's go!"

The girls stood and quickly checked their surroundings. "Go!" exhaled Ava.

Crouched low, they ran to the side of the building.

"We're down thirty seconds," said Carol, ticking off the time in her head.

Ava's heart beat like the drum of a heavy metal band. Even though she knew they had about three more minutes, she couldn't help looking over her shoulders every two seconds.

Carol lifted the board vertically and leaned it against the wall. "Hold the bottom secure!" she said firmly.

"Got it." Ava crouched down and gripped the makeshift ladder.

Carol didn't hesitate. She carefully stepped onto the first wooden board and slowly made her way to the top. Once her shoulders were level with the bottom of the fire escape, she grabbed the support bars. Then, while moving her feet to the top of the ladder, she pulled herself to safety. She looked at her watch. "Two minutes, Ava," she called out. "Hurry!"

Carol lay flush on the cold metal floor of the fire escape. She grabbed the top of the ladder as Ava began climbing. "You got this," Ava whispered as she fought to stop her hands and feet from shaking her right off the ladder. Her brain ping-ponged between *you're gonna make it* and *you're gonna fall and break every bone in your body.*

"Come on!" Carol encouraged her. "You've got this. Come on!"

The board wobbled and bowed as she climbed, but finally, Ava arrived at the top. She grabbed the fire escape, and with Carol's help, she pulled herself to safety.

They grabbed the ladder and pulled it onto the platform with them. "One minute left," Carol whispered. In the distance, they could see the golf cart's light making its orbit of the parking lot.

Carol placed the ladder against the building and began climbing to the rooftop. A few seconds later, she was on the roof looking down at Ava.

Ava glanced over her shoulder. It was too late—the golf cart was heading their way! "They're here!" whispered Ava, panicking.

"Ava, get on that board and climb NOW!" hissed Carol through clenched teeth.

Ava grasped the bottom of the ladder. She looked over her shoulder—the cart was about fifty feet away and rapidly closing in. Ava concentrated—one hand at a time, one foot at a time. She looked up when she felt Carol's hand around her wrist.

"Come on!" whispered Carol urgently.

The guard was out of the cart. He shone his flashlight at the dumpster, then turned the beam toward the fire escape. "The ladder!" whispered Carol, her eyes wide with panic.

Ava grabbed the ladder and jerked it upward. The bottom banged the metal railing of the fire escape. Both guards were out of the cart now, shining their lights upward. Ava and Carol lay perfectly still, not daring to look over the ledge. Their makeshift ladder lay beside them.

They could hear them talking and see the guards' flashlights probing the fire escape and the side of the building. It seemed like an eternity, but finally the guards seemed satisfied that nothing was amiss… and drove off.

Ava crept slowly to the edge of the building and looked down. "They're gone," she whispered. A look of relief washed over Carol's face.

"That was close!" Carol said.

"Too close," Ava breathed. Her entire body was trembling. She stared at the sky—a narrow strand of clouds stretched like taffy across the moon. She took a moment to control her breathing. Carol was motioning her to follow her. Ava uttered up a small prayer of thanks and then took off across the rooftop.

Carol stopped and knelt in front of a shiny metallic structure that looked like a small house. "According to the blueprints, this is the ventilation system that will lead me to the room with the safe," said Carol matter-of-factly.

"Be careful…," said Ava quietly, her face filled with concern. "Just like at the museum… I'll stay in touch with you by phone."

"I will," said Carol. Ava helped her fasten the GoPro on her head, and then clipped a small penlight to the side of the head strap.

"Oh my God, Carol," said Ava, "you look just like a spy!"

"I feel like a spy, or a spelunker. I'm going to go with spy." She unscrewed the eight screws that secured the aluminum housing to the rooftop. The vent was pitch black, but plenty wide for Carol's tall, narrow frame.

Ava helped Carol scoot into the opening to the ventilation system. "Good luck," said Ava. She tried to hide the worry in her voice.

Carol looked up, smiled, and gave Ava a thumbs-up. "They'll never know I was here!" She spread her legs to brace herself, wedged her feet against the aluminum walls of the duct system, and began slowly lowering herself downward.

A million thoughts ran through Carol's mind as she descended. She knew that the ventilation system was only about forty feet long, but it seemed like it was a mile. The duct system ran downward at a manageable angle, and then for the last eight feet, dropped nearly straight down.

Carol wedged her arms and her feet against the walls of the duct and slowly maneuvered herself down to where the ventilation system made the eight-foot vertical drop. Wedging her sneakers against the sides of the shaft, she slowly shifted her bodyweight from side to side, inching down until she finally reached the bottom.

She sat quietly, listening. She had done her best to be silent on her descent, but it wasn't easy, especially when you combine rubber-soled sneakers and aluminum. But all was quiet. She gently pulled out her phone and whispered, "I made it. Everything is okay!"

Ava let out a sigh of relief when she heard Carol's voice. She had been crawling along the rooftop, keeping track of the security detail and watching to see if any other visitors arrived. So far, except for the very predictable orbit of the security guards, all else was quiet.

Carol crouched down in front of the air-conditioning vent and listened. The secure room was silent and dark, except for a bright red light that stared at her like a cyclops. Using her penlight, she counted six screws. "Okay," she whispered as she wiped her hands off on her pants. She slowly unscrewed the first screw. *That was easy*. She held the screw in her left hand and was starting on the second when she heard footsteps approaching. She flicked off her penlight and closed her eyes as the room was flooded with powerful, bright fluorescent lights.

She listened intently, willing her heart to slow down. The door to the room whooshed open and men's voices filled the air. She heard a heavy thud followed by the sound of a metallic locking device.

"The Captain will be proud," laughed a deep voice. "A priceless piano, Chopin's last handwritten concerto, and the coup de grâce, the Ramesses diamonds." Carol silently pressed the *Record* button on the GoPro.

"The piano is absolutely gorgeous, a spectacular piece," said a high, nasally voice.

Carol scrunched down as much as humanly possible and peaked through the vent. She could see four men in the room. A tall, wispy man in a dark suit, with black hair streaked with silver, was rubbing his hand across the piano. She guessed the high-pitched voice belonged to him.

Another man, whom Carol guessed was the second man from the Mercedes, was grinning from ear to ear. His bald head glistened like a light bulb in the brightly lit room.

Carol silently removed the GoPro from her head and aligned it with an opening in the vent. She could have kicked herself—she missed the part where they had talked about Ramesses's diamonds.

"The piano itself is worth close to ten million dollars," said the deep-voiced man, "and the concerto should easily fetch close to a million."

"All incredibly amazing and appreciated," said the nasally man. "I was told you have an ingenious plan for delivering the diamonds?"

"Ah, yes," laughed the deep-voiced man. He smiled mischievously. "You see, this piano comes with a secret."

Carol could see the man with the deep voice clearly now. He wore a charcoal gray suit that matched his salt-and-pepper, closely shaved hair.

"You see," he laughed, "Chopin's last concerto will actually deliver the diamonds to your client."

Carol watched the thin man's face fill with confusion. "I'm not sure what you mean."

"George, show Mr. Snow our little secret."

Carol gasped as a man sat at the piano. She recognized him from the museum. It was George, the security guard!

"Yes, Mr. Roach."

George sat at the piano and played a series of notes: *da, da, da, da, dah, dah, dah, duh, da, da, da, da duh.* Suddenly, a tiny drawer about the size of a cell phone slid open.

"Just let the Captain know that he merely needs to play the first thirteen notes of the concerto, and his diamonds will appear," smiled Mr. Roach. George gently tapped the front of the drawer, and it slid back into place.

"That's brilliant," gasped Mr. Snow.

"The hidden mechanism is so perfectly designed that it will not show up on any x-ray. It'll merely look like the innerworkings of the piano."

"This is perfect," gasped the nasally guest, clasping his hand in delight. "And the diamonds... they are safe?"

"Yes, the diamonds will be inside a foam pouch made of high-Z foam, which actually blocks and scatters x-rays. We are taking every precaution necessary to protect them."

"So, the diamonds will be hidden in the piano when you transport it to the auction tomorrow?" asked the bald man, needing reassurance.

"When we deliver the piano and the other items to the private auction tomorrow, everything will be in place for immediate shipment. We'll place the diamonds in the piano before everything is moved to the armored car tomorrow. Tell the Captain that we have arranged for a direct flight of a cargo jet from Hanscom Airport to a private airstrip in Ireland."

"I will let the Captain know. He will be most pleased," said the nasally man, his voice quivering with excitement.

"I'm sure he will," said the deep-voiced man. "Shall we?" he said, motioning toward the door.

The group of men walked toward the door. There was a loud metallic click and then a whoosh as the door swung open. "When can we expect delivery?" Carol wasn't sure who the voice belonged to. She thought it sounded like the bald man.

Just before the door slammed shut, she heard someone say, "We're leaving at noon." Carol sat motionless, waiting another few seconds, and then turned on her penlight. She had everything she needed.

Ava jumped when she heard Carol's voice. "I'm on my way," she whispered breathily.

Ava closed her eyes. Those were the best four words she'd ever heard! "Awesome. Climb carefully!" she whispered, her voice filled with excitement. The electronic *chirp, chirp* of a car unlocking made Ava jump. She quickly traversed the rooftop in a semi-crouch position, not because she had to, but because she thought it looked cool.

Cautiously, she peered over the edge. The super-sleek security golf cart had pulled to a halt in the parking lot. The two guards watched as the Mercedes backed up and pulled away. The guard at the wheel touched his ear. Ava was close enough to hear, "They've left. All's clear." Then, with a high-pitched whine, the golf cart pulled away from the curb to begin another orbit around the auction house.

"Ava," a voice whispered.

Ava jumped back from the edge of the building. She clutched her heart. She was pretty sure it had leapt out of her body and was sprinting away to safety without her. She whirled around to find Carol crouched down behind her. "Geesh, what are you, part cat? I didn't even hear you."

Carol put her hand on her friend's shoulder. "Ava," she whispered breathlessly, "they have the diamonds."

"What? Wait, you saw them? Did you get the diamonds?!" she asked, grabbing her friend's shoulders excitedly.

"No, listen! They're going to hide them in a secret compartment in Chopin's piano."

"That's crazy," Ava whispered. "Then it *is* the dude from Ireland. So, he'll buy the piano at auction, the diamonds will be inside, then it's shipped to him in Ireland?"

"Yes, and since he knows that there are millions of dollars in the piano, he'll feel comfortable outbidding everyone else."

"You've got to admit, it's a pretty good way to smuggle goods out of the U.S."

"Oh, I almost forgot, they refer to the billionaire in Ireland as the Captain."

"Captain?" snorted Ava, rolling her eyes. "For real?"

"It's horrible, I know," Carol smiled.

"We've solved the case, Big Brain. I think we should call the police?"

"Eh… We will…," Carol paused.

"I know that pause," said Ava, giving her an apprehensive look.

"Hear me out. I have a good reason to wait. They're going to hide the diamonds in the piano, right?"

Ava nodded, "According to what you heard."

"Then, they're putting the piano in an armored car. I think that when the piano is safe in the armored car, that's when we bring the cavalry in."

Ava thought for a moment. "I see what you're saying," she agreed. "It's easy for the bad guys to hide something small in a building this big."

Carol nodded in agreement. "Right. If it's safe and secure in the armored truck, there's less chance of them vanishing again."

"So, what's our next move?"

"I'm working on that, but right now we have a bigger problem." Carol looked over the edge of the building. "How are you at climbing down?"

Ava took in a deep breath and glanced back at their makeshift ladder. "Honestly, I'd rather gargle canned tuna fish water."

The girls crept silently to the ledge just above the fire escape and waited for their favorite two guards. They lay on their stomachs, chins resting on their palms, peering over the edge of the building.

"They have the most boring job ever," whispered Carol as they watched them check behind the dumpster and the fire escape.

"They live their lives in three-minute increments. That means they circle this building twenty times an hour. One hundred sixty times in an eight-hour shift."

"They're gone. Come on! You can be scared later." And just like that, the game of cat and mouse began.

Carol held the ladder in place as Ava shakily descended to the safety of the fire escape. She returned the favor for Carol, who called down, "Two minutes!" over her shoulder as she descended.

Ava edged the ladder against the building… then watched horrified as it wobbled and fell with a loud *thud* sound to the ground. "Oh my God!" she whispered.

Carol looked at Ava, her eyes opened wide. "Our ladder! What happened?"

"It must have been on a rock or hole or something…. I couldn't see anything—it just fell."

Carol looked at her watch. "One and a half minutes!"

"Carol," said Ava, "how far is it down?"

"At least twelve feet!"

"I'm five feet. Can you drop from seven feet?"

"All day every day. Why?"

Ava climbed over the railing of the fire escape. She maneuvered until she was hanging from the bottom. "Ava, you're crazy!" shrieked Carol.

"It's seven feet from my feet to the ground. You said seven feet all day every day. Now come on!"

Ava took in a deep breath and dropped. The impact was harsh, but she relaxed her knees, fell forward and rolled. Her palms stung as they hit the pavement, but her arms were saved by the sleeves of her hoodie.

"Come on, Carol. I'll help spot you. Hurry, they are going to be here any second!" Carol climbed over the railing. This time it was *her* turn to be shaky.

Ava saw the lights from the golf cart as it started its first turn at the end of the parking lot. In a matter of seconds, it would make a beeline toward them.

"Carol, NOW!" shouted Ava through clenched teeth.

Carol dropped as Ava threw her arms around her, hoping to help slow her descent. Instead, it felt like Carol had just torn her arms out of their sockets as they both sprawled forward onto the ground.

"Ow!" moaned Carol. "I could have done without the spot."

"You're welcome," said Ava. "I'm putting you in remedial jumping classes if we ever get out of here alive!"

Carol and Ava's heads swiveled simultaneously— the golf cart was making its final turn. "We're trapped," said Carol, panicking.

"No!" shouted Ava. "Grab the ladder—you and I are about to make our cross-country coach proud!"

Carol grabbed the ladder and took off after Ava. The golf cart was getting closer. They raced along the side of the building, barely staying ahead of the headlights. They slid around the corner behind the building just as the cart came to a stop.

"They're going to check the dumpster and the fire escape," gasped Carol. "We've just got to make it back to our hiding place."

Ava grabbed the ladder from Carol. "Let's do this."

The girls clung to the shadows of the building, running as quietly as possible while carrying a ten-foot ladder.

They paused at the front of the building, gasping for air, their lungs burning. The parking lot was so bright it looked like daytime. Carol reached over and grabbed the ladder from Ava.

"My turn!" panted Carol. Ava gladly relinquished the ladder.

They raced across the parking lot to their hiding spot just as the cart came around the far corner of the building. Breathless, the girls sat and watched the golf cart complete another loop. A thought hit Ava as the guard checked behind the dumpster and then checked the fire escape. "We should have just thrown the ladder—"

"In the dumpster," interrupted Carol with a laugh. "I thought of that too."

Ava picked up her favorite ladder, and the girls quickly crossed the street. "If you don't mind," smiled Ava, "I'm going to leave your creation here until tomorrow."

"Please," said Carol. "Good riddance!"

Ava checked her phone for texts from her parents—there were none. She let out a sigh of relief. Her eyes moved to the top of the screen. It was 11:30 p.m.

"Let's get back to the tent just in case my parents check on us," said Ava. "Then, we can work on our plan of attack."

"We should also try to get a little sleep or else we'll be dead tomorrow," Carol said, "and we'll need our wits about us."

"I need all the wits I can get," smiled Ava as she climbed onto her bike. "Let's go!"

11
FINESSE, NOT FITNESS

"Down, down," whispered Ava as the shadow slowly approached their tent.

The girls quickly sprawled on top of their sleeping bags, pretending to sleep. They had made it back just in time. Five minutes earlier, Ava's father would have found an empty tent.

He pulled the mosquito netting down over the front of the tent, and as quietly as possible, zipped it closed. The girls looked tuckered out. He smiled to himself, remembering when he was young. He paused and looked at a couple of the moon sketches they had laid out for Ava's parents (a ruse just in case they got curious). He took one more look at the girls, and then disappeared back inside the house.

Ava and Carol lay quietly for a few moments, listening. Ava sat up and looked at the house. All the lights were off.

"Okay," whispered Ava, sitting up. "What's the plan, Super Brain?"

Carol raised her hand to her mouth as she yawned. "I can tell you what we *need* to make happen. However, making it happen may take a little finesse."

"I think I've had all the finesse I can take, between biking a gazillion miles, climbing, not to mention sprinting with a huge wooden contraption."

"Finesse, Ava, not fitness. It means tweaking."

"Why didn't you just say tweaking?"

"Because it's more like careful tweaking, like skillfully changing something. Why does it matter? What matters is the thieves are moving the piano with the diamonds to a secret location at noon tomorrow."

Ava nodded, covering her mouth with her hand as she yawned, making a *go on* gesture with the other.

"So, my plan is to get some sleep. Then call the police at the perfect time to stop the armored truck. Otherwise, we may spook the bad guys. Everything is going to require impeccable timing."

"You have proof on the GoPro, so I guess convincing them shouldn't be too difficult."

"I have compelling evidence… unfortunately, it was illegally obtained. I was thinking that I could send it to the police anonymously, but the problem is, everything has to be timed perfectly. We need the police to be at the auction house just as the bad guys are about to pull out."

Ava nodded. "If the police get there too early, the bad guys will be able to hide the diamonds. If they get there too late, the thieves will vanish to some unknown location."

"Exactly," nodded Carol.

Ava felt her eyes closing. She shook her head, trying to stay awake.

"I'm setting the alarm for eight-thirty," Carol opened the clock app on her phone. "That'll give us about six hours of sleep."

Ava muttered something unintelligible, her face already buried in her pillow. Carol laid back on her sleeping bag and closed her eyes. A cyclone of thoughts whipped around her brain. *There's no way I'm falling asleep tonight…* and then she did.

12
THE CAPTAIN'S CHOPIN FOR A PIANO

Ava jerked awake to Carol's phone, belting out master bassoonist Klaus Thunemann's version of "Flight of the Bumblebee." "Make it stop. Please…," whimpered Ava as she folded her pillow around her head.

"Ahh," sighed Carol. "The bassoon sounds so playful and frolicsome, don't you think? *Frisky* comes to mind. I think he captures the spirit of the bumblebee in flight, don't you?"

"I think he has captured the sound of every hope and every dream I've ever had leaving my body." Ava rolled over and glared at Carol, "Why are you so perky this morning? Be angry, like me."

"It just so happens that while you were enjoying your beauty sleep, I came up with a plan."

"Does the plan involve a brush? I've got a seriously bad combo of helmet hair and bed head, with a touch of crazy."

"We're going to need to do some reconnaissance this morning. We'll need eyes on the auction house." Ava moaned and sat up. "Oh my," said Carol, grabbing her phone and excitedly jabbing at the screen.

"What is it?" asked Ava, fully awake now.

"Animal Planet. They can stop searching—I've found Bigfoot!"

"You are so funny," Ava laughed, smacking Carol with her pillow.

"Okay, we've got three hours to pull all this together."

"All right," said Ava as she ripped a phone through her tangles. "What did you come up with?"

"Well, we know we can't call the police too early or too late. That means we have to be there. We need to see them put the piano in the truck."

"I kind of expected that," said Ava. "I figured we would have to be on site to let the police know when to leap into action."

"The problem is," said Carol, "the loading docks are in the back of the building."

"We're a couple of kids—no one is going to be paying any attention to us. We could just be hanging out."

"No, George might spot us," said Carol.

"George? The security guard from the museum?" Ava asked, thoroughly confused.

"That's right, I forgot to tell you!" said Carol excitedly. "George was there last night. He played the piano to open the hidden compartment."

"Hmm, makes sense now. I thought that his hands were extremely soft for a hardened criminal."

Carol grabbed Ava's laptop and flipped it open. She typed in the address for the auction company and clicked the map icon. "Bingo! There's a Starbucks directly behind it!" she exclaimed.

"Perfect," said Ava with a nod. "We can get breakfast, decaf mochas, and surveil the building at the same time."

"We'll wait until they begin loading the truck and then call the police. Middleville only has a population of about ten thousand people. It can't take the police more than five minutes to get anywhere in that town."

It was 10 a.m. by the time the girls had jumped on their bikes and raced toward Starbucks to set up their secret observation post. They both turned and stared at the Prestige Auction building as they pedaled by. Who would have guessed that one of the largest heists in history had occurred right here in this quiet little town?

The Starbucks parking lot was packed. For a moment, the girls panicked, wondering if they would find a seat. Luckily, it was a nice day, so they were able to find a table at the outdoor patio. A giant metal fence was all that separated them from Prestige's parking lot.

"It's weird," said Carol as she stared at the fence and beyond.

"What's weird?" asked Ava. "My natural beauty? My charisma?"

"Sure," Carol smiled, "that was exactly what I was thinking."

"I thought so," Ava laughed.

"I just think it's interesting that while everyone is sitting around enjoying their café lattes—with their faces buried in their phones—not more than one hundred feet away, stolen diamonds are about to—" Carol stopped talking. Ava stopped drinking her mocha—a large, armored truck had just pulled up to the gate.

"George," whispered Ava as she watched the tall, lanky driver jump out of the truck and jab at a security keypad on the gate.

Moments later, the armored truck rumbled to the back of the building. Ava and Carol recognized the logo: Mona Lisa mocked them with a smug, self-confident grin.

The truck beeped as it backed up to the loading dock. The brakes sighed squeakily, and the truck shuddered, coming to a stop in front of a large outcrop of cement, covered by rubber that looked like a giant car bumper. A large, metallic door at the back of the building began to noisily clank upward.

"I can't see anything!" said Carol anxiously. "The truck's blocking our view."

"Come on!" said Ava as she grabbed Carol's arm and dragged her from her seat.

The girls ran through the parking lot and then up the sidewalk that ran parallel to the Prestige auction building. They stopped alongside the fence when they were directly across from the loading dock.

"Get down, there's George," said Carol quietly as the tall security guard appeared at the back of the truck. The girls crouched behind a trashcan. "If we can see him, he can see us," Carol warned.

"Yeah, I understand how eyes work," Ava replied.

Carol dropped to her knees and peaked around the edge of the trashcan. "We're way too obvious. If anyone pulls up, they're going to know we're up to something. Plus, I can barely see anything from here."

"I have an idea. Grab your phone." Ava pulled her phone out of her pocket, and then motioned Carol to lean in closer. "Thank you," said Ava, pulling the drawstring out of Carol's hoodie.

"Why would you do that?"

"I needed it."

"You have a hoodie too, you know?"

"Use my own? Do you know how hard it is to restring these things? Can I see your phone?"

"Absolutely not," Carol gripped it tightly against her.

"Fine." Ava casually walked over to the "No Parking" sign that was located next to the fence surrounding the Prestige Auction building. Using the string from Carol's hoodie, she tied it in place, then called Carol on FaceTime. She waited until Carol answered, then smiled into the camera. "Now you can see the docking bay."

"Look," Carol said when Ava returned.

Three men dressed in blue overalls stood beside George on the delivery dock. George unlocked the back of the truck and raised the door.

"Looks like they're about to load the piano. Carol, you gotta call the police."

"I know." Carol's heart was pounding. "But if they show up too soon, the diamonds could be gone forever. We have to time this just right."

George leaned lazily against the back of the truck playing with the ends of his mustache. The three men were no longer on the dock.

"Look at him, not a care in the world. I wonder what it's like to not have a conscience."

"Once he's arrested, perhaps you can ask him," suggested Carol.

"I wonder if they'll put his massive mustache in handcuffs too."

"There's the piano," whispered Carol. The piano was completely covered in thick moving blankets. Foam padding covered the edges. The team of men in their blue uniforms were carefully maneuvering it on several dollies to the back of the truck. Carol's heart was pounding. Ava gave her a *what are you waiting for* look.

George and one of the workmen jumped onto the back of the truck while the other men cautiously moved the piano inch by inch into the bed of the truck.

"Alright," said Carol, "it's showtime." Her hands shook as she Googled Middleville Police and hit the call button.

The call was answered immediately by an extremely bored-sounding man. "Middleville Police Dispatch. How may I help you?"

"Hi, I'm calling about the diamonds that were stolen from the Hancock Museum. We know where they are." Carol felt like she was gasping for breath.

"Who am I speaking with?"

"Carol Miller. Sir, we don't have much time. They're being shipped out of the Prestige Auction Company. Please hurry."

The dispatcher's voice rapidly turned from bored to agitated. "Young lady. You do know that filing a false police report—"

"Look, I'm telling you that they have the diamonds and if you don't hurry and send…. Hello? Hello?" Carol turned to Ava completely dismayed. "He hung up on me."

Ava kept her mouth shut—she knew this was no time for an *I told you so*. She needed to figure out what to do, and fast. Then it hit her, Detective Edwards. "Carol, give me your phone. I have an idea—I'm most likely going to be grounded until I'm married, but it's gotta be done." Without a question, Carol handed her phone over. Ava jabbed in the number that her mother had made her memorize in case there was ever an emergency. She hoped for her and Carol's sake, this constituted as one of those times.

The phone rang three times before a gruff voice answered the phone. Detective Edwards.

"Mr. Edwards? It's me, Ava!" Her heart was beating so hard, she was sure he could hear it through the phone.

"Ava, are you okay?" Concern immediately filled his voice.

"Yes and no. Please listen and please believe me. I know where the diamonds are that were stolen from the museum!"

"Ava." His voice was tinged with anger. "You know that this number is *only* for emergencies...."

"Mr. Edwards, I'm not playing. You can be angry at me later, but if you don't hurry, the diamonds are going to be gone forever. We have video, we can prove it, you *have* to believe me." Ava felt dizzy as the words tumbled out of her mouth.

"Ava, where are you?" he demanded.

"We're hiding at the side of the Prestige Auction building. They've hidden the diamonds in a piano and they're about to leave."

Ava could hear the *ding, ding* of the detective's car door.

"How do you know the diamonds are in the piano? Did you see them? Ava, *did* you see them put them in there?" His voice was a mixture of frustration and concern.

"Please, Blake." Ava could feel tears of frustration coming to her eyes. "Trust me. I would never lie to you—please hurry."

"I trust you, Ava. You're just like your mother," he sighed. "Get away from the building and get to a safe place. I'm on my way."

"He's on his way," said Ava. She hurried over to the "No Parking" sign and retrieved her phone.

"They're closing the back of the truck," said Carol in a panic. "If he doesn't hurry, they're gonna get away!"

George climbed into the truck and started the engine. A huge plume of gray-white smoke billowed from the exhaust pipe. He stuck his hand out the window and gave the workmen a thumbs-up.

"This is a nightmare," declared Carol. "What do we do?"

"We could stand in front of the gate—they'd never run over us," said Ava, who was running out of ideas.

"Are you kidding? They have millions of dollars in diamonds in that truck. I don't know what they would do."

"You got a better plan?" She looked at Carol and didn't wait for an answer. She took off for the gate as the truck pulled away from the loading dock. "Come on!" she yelled.

The girls sprinted down the sidewalk as the huge white truck drove along the building, parallel to them. George turned the wheel and headed straight toward the gate.

"Make yourself look huge and menacing!" Ava cried out.

"It's a huge truck—I doubt we'd even dent his grill."

George pulled up to the gate and screeched to a stop. He jumped from the driver's side, said something to his companion and calmly walked up to the keypad to open the gate.

"Hi George, long time no see," said Ava. "How's the museum?"

George's jaw dropped. He scowled at them, quickly regaining his composure. "You two. What are you doing here?"

"I wanted to let you know we found a mate for your mustache. A friendly sea lion named Sualia."

"George, what's going on?" shouted a squat man from the passenger seat. George held up his hand signaling *just a second.* "I should have done away with you two when I had the chance." He pulled his phone out of his pocket. "Now scram before I call the police."

"No need to do that," said Carol, crossing her arms. "We've already called them. They should be here in minute now."

George eyed them suspiciously and then sneered. "Liars." He flung the door open, jumped into the truck and gunned the engine. The truck lurched toward the girls.

Ava and Carol clenched their jaws and held their ground. George's companion punched the dash and jumped out of the truck. Ava's eyes widened. The man looked like a human bowling ball—he was as wide as he was tall.

"Either you move," he said with a thick New England accent, "or I'm gonna permanently move you." He smiled, showing a mouth filled with broken, decayed teeth. Carol wished he'd saved his smile for someone else… like the dentist.

"Suit yourself!" he said angrily.

He grabbed Carol by the arm. She spun toward him, kicking him as hard as she could in the shins. Ava charged him, swinging her backpack like a ball and chain at his head.

He grabbed her backpack and hauled her in. The girls began screaming "Help!" at the top of their lungs. Carol flung her head backward as hard as she could, catching the man square in the nose. There was a loud *crack*!

"Argh!" screamed the man, who fell back while grabbing his face. Suddenly they were free!

Ava spun around and kicked the man in the unmentionables. His eyes rolled up in his head. He made a high-pitched whistling sound like a tea kettle going off as he crumpled to the ground.

"Way to go, foot!" whispered Ava.

A black police SUV came flying over the hill, blue lights flashing in the grill. George no longer seemed to care if he ran over the girls or not. He put the truck in gear and began to pull forward.

"No you don't!" yelled Ava. She flung off her backpack, dragged out the Thor 2000 and pointed it directly at George. The high-powered light struck him in the face like a laser beam. He threw up his forearm to protect his eyes, but it was too late. The truck accelerated forward just missing the girls as they dove out of the way. It flew across the street, hopped the curb, and crashed into a cluster of trees and bushes.

George kicked the door open and leapt from the truck. He tried to get away, but the Thor 2000 had done its job. Still blinded, he ran straight into a tree, and then another tree. He teetered awkwardly and then fell to the ground, clutching his forehead. He moaned as another police cruiser came flying over the hill.

A dark-haired man in a grey suit with the build of a football player ran toward them. He grabbed the girls by the shoulders. "Are you okay?" He quickly eyed them from head to toe.

"Yes. Yes, thank you, Mr. Edwards." She pointed to George, "He's the security guard from the

Hancock Museum. And the human bowling ball," Detective Edwards looked in the direction Ava was pointing, "is one of his accomplices."

Detective Edwards gestured toward the rotund man, who was running down the sidewalk toward Starbucks. Two officers took off in pursuit after him.

"The diamonds are in the back of the truck," said Ava. "We couldn't call you until we knew they were there—because if we waited for you to get a warrant...."

"And the building is so big," added Carol. "We were worried they would hide or move the diamonds—and then they would be gone forever."

"It's okay, it's okay," said Detective Edwards, holding up his hand. "You two, over by my car— and..." he held up a warning finger, "do not move."

Two more police cruisers arrived on the scene. Across the Prestige Auction parking lot, a silver-haired man in a three-piece suit was making his way toward them in a golfcart.

"What do you think you're doing?" he cried, shaking his fist in the air. "This is private property. I'll have your badge."

"And you are?" asked Detective Edwards calmly.

"Renaldo White III. Owner of Prestige Auctions, taxpayer and friend of the mayor."

"Delightful. I'm Detective Edwards and I have a few questions for you. Is that your truck?" He pointed to the large, armored vehicle across the street.

Renaldo's jaw dropped. "What have you done? Do you realize that there is a piano worth millions of dollars inside?"

"I'm less concerned about the piano and more concerned that your driver attempted to run over these two girls. And his crony physically accosted them." Renaldo looked at George and the short squat man with disgust.

"Have you heard of attempted vehicular homicide, Mr. White?"

"I have," he gave Detective Edwards a surly smile. "Girls, I apologize." He turned his attention back to Detective Edwards. "These men are simply hired help. They broke the law—do what you need to do," he waved dismissively.

"Mr. White," stammered George in disbelief, "Do something!"

"I'm sorry, George," Renaldo brushed his hands together as if dusting them off. "It's out of my hands. However, I do have very good lawyers," he gave George a knowing look.

"Mr. White," Detective Edwards snapped his fingers to get his attention. "Since your truck was involved in a crime, and a crash, we're going to need to take a look at the vehicle."

"I think not. The two men were clearly in the wrong. However, the contents of the truck are not to be involved in the investigation. We're talking about historical artifacts worth millions."

"Then perhaps you should make wiser hiring decisions. Especially in this case, since the vehicle was used as a weapon. So yes, we will be examining the *contents* of the truck." Mr. White turned red with anger. "You," said Detective Edwards to George. "Where are the keys?"

"Don't answer him, George," snarled Mr. White.

"Mr. White, you are interfering with a police investigation," said Detective Edwards hotly. He pointed to a tall officer with fiery red hair. "Handcuff Mr. White."

"They're… they're in the truck," stammered George.

"Thank you, George." Detective Edwards trudged over to the cab of the truck, climbed inside, and retrieved the keys. He searched through the keyring and found the correct key to unlock the back of the truck. Chopin's piano sat entombed in blue moving cloths.

"Ava," he called over his shoulder, "you said the diamonds were hidden in the piano?"

"Diamonds? This is preposterous!" screamed Mr. White, his face as pale as his name.

"Yes," said Carol, answering for Ava. "She has to play the first thirteen notes of Chopin's last piano concerto—then a secret drawer will open."

"Don't touch that piano! It's worth millions!" screamed Mr. White.

"We know," said Detective Edwards. "I believe you've told us a million times."

Ava climbed up into the truck and delicately removed the packing materials protecting the piano. Carol handed Ava her phone—she had loaded the first two measures of Chopin's concerto.

"See?" smiled Carol. "All those years of piano practice are about to come in handy."

"Maybe someday someone will hide something in a bassoon, and you can blow it out," smiled Ava wryly.

"You have such a way with words."

"Okay, here we go." Ava's hands trembled as she touched the piano, Chopin's piano. She took in a deep breath and exhaled in an attempt to calm her nerves. All was quiet as Ava gently tapped out the thirteen notes, just as Chopin had done on this very piano two hundred years ago.

When she hit the thirteenth note, everyone gasped as a small drawer slid open. Ava reached in and removed a small cloth pouch. Every mouth dropped as she carefully poured the contents onto her palm. She and Carol had saved Ramesses's royal diamonds.

13
DO THEY HAVE KNOCK-KNOCK JOKES IN IRELAND?

The FBI stepped in and took over the investigation. Two undercover agents disguised as Prestige Auction drivers delivered the piano and other auction goods to the private auction, then left, according to plan.

Mr. White was told he would get a much lighter sentence if he called and told the people at the private auction everything was okay and right on schedule. He knew he had lost and was cooperating fully with the FBI.

He also sent the Captain a special email with an attachment called "The Last Concerto." Mr. White told the Captain that the first thirteen notes of the concerto would be of great benefit to all who listened.

What the Captain didn't know was that the FBI had embedded an untraceable virus into the PDF attachment. Once the attachment was opened, the virus would allow the FBI to hack into his private network. This would be the beginning of the end for the Captain.

That evening, the auction went off without a hitch. The private broker made the purchases for the Captain. Chopin's piano and the handwritten concerto were loaded onto a plane to leave for a private airstrip owned by the Captain in Ireland. The broker contacted the Captain and told him he would have a *sparkling* morning.

Ava and Carol asked for one *small* favor from the FBI. "I mean," said Ava to the lead investigator, "We did crack the case for you and made you aware of a hidden network of investors."

The FBI agreed of course. Ava and Carol were allowed to send a little present to the Captain.

Waterford, Ireland – Dragon's Point Airstrip

The Captain sat in his private library filled with famous paintings, sculptures, rare books, and an incredibly ornate stand carved out of pure ivory upon which sat a glass box with a plush velvet cushion. It was created for something very special.

Tonight, he wore his black linen pants, a cardigan sweater, and a blood-red smoking jacket. He picked up his cigar and drew in a long drag. Smoke billowed from his nostrils like a dragon.

His leathery tan face broke into a narrow slit of a smile as six men arrived, carefully carrying Chopin's piano into his library. He leapt to his feet with surprising agility and pointed to an empty corner. The men cautiously carried the piano to the designated area, then bowed to the Captain, who shooed them away with his cigar. They quickly and quietly left the room, closing the door behind them.

The Captain stared at the piano and ran his hand across the wood. He breathed in deeply, his nostrils filled with the scent of history. Reverently, he sat at the piano and closed his eyes. He had printed the music that Mr. White had emailed him, and being an accomplished musician, he only glanced at the sheet of music before setting it aside. Now, sitting at the piano, he needed only to touch the keys. The melody flowed from his fingertips.

As the notes rang out, filling the room, a hidden drawer slid open. He looked down at the satin bag and then at his beautiful ornate display case. *Yes*, he thought, *my collection will be complete.*

With a quivering hand, he reached down and grasped the bag. He carefully opened it and poured the contents into his palm. He stared and shook his head. His brain couldn't catch up with what his eyes were seeing. In his hand lay five children's marbles… and a handwritten note.

Vitriol filled his veins as he read.

Knock-knock.

Who's there?

Jewel.

Jewel who?

Jewel never get Ramesses's diamonds.

"You'll pay!" the Captain screamed, leaping from the piano. "You'll pay!"

14
A MIGHTY HUGE CHECK

Ava and Carol stood on the stone steps of the Hancock Museum and waved to a crowd of journalists and photographers. Overnight, the girls had turned into local celebrities.

"I could live like this," Ava sighed. "All of this adoration and adulation."

"It is surreal," acknowledged Carol. She spotted Gladys in the crowd and bumped Ava's shoulder. "There's Gladys!" They both waved excitedly at their new friend, who was beaming up at them. Feedback from a microphone grabbed everyone's attention.

"Sorry about that, folks," said a thin man in an impeccable gray suit. "Thank you everyone for coming out today. On behalf of the Hancock Museum, it is my esteemed honor to present Ava Clarke and Carol Miller this check for $10,000. Thanks to your investigative genius and courage, you have solved one of the largest jewel heists in American history!" Ava and Carol waved to the crowd and graciously accepted the check. Ava wondered how they were possibly going to fit it in the ATM.

The next morning, Ava and Carol stopped by the museum. Gladys looked up from the reception desk, her eyes filled with joy. "My two investigators!" she exclaimed. She rushed from behind the counter and gave them both a hug.

"We couldn't have done it without you, Gladys!" said Carol.

"We wanted to stop by and thank you for saving us, and for believing in us," smiled Ava.

"We're also sorry it wasn't under other circumstances," Carol gave an embarrassed smile.

"What in the world are you talking about?" Gladys clucked her tongue. "You two have single-handedly made the Hancock Museum more popular than ever. The phone hasn't stopped ringing." Ava looked at the phone, which wasn't ringing and arched an eyebrow. "Well, that figures," laughed Gladys.

"I guess we better get going," Ava sighed, glancing out the museum doors. "My parents are outside waiting for us. Just so you know, it may be years before you see us again."

"Your parents are that angry?" asked Gladys.

"My mom said that I couldn't leave my room until I was old enough to go to college."

"She did, did she?" Gladys crossed her arms, a mischievous look in her eyes. "Did your mother ever tell you about the Larson train robbery or the famous Middleton pickpocket?"

"No...," Ava eyed Glady's curiously. "Was she somehow involved?"

"Involved? Your mother was knee-deep investigating the crimes. Her shenanigans nearly drove your grandfather crazy. But…," she looked at Ava and Carol kindly, "I know that he was proud of her."

"Did Mrs. Clarke solve the crimes?" asked Carol.

"She did, and many others. So, don't let your mom be too hard on you, and maybe ask her to tell you about Larson's or the Middleton pickpocket."

"I will," smiled Ava. A feeling of pride swept over her. "My mom must have been one cool kid."

"She sure was," Gladys agreed. The phone rang, making them jump.

"I guess that's our cue," said Carol. They waved goodbye and headed for the door, ready for their next adventure.

AVA & CAROL
DETECTIVE AGENCY

Thank you for reading *The Mystery of the Pharaoh's Diamonds*

Sign up for info on upcoming books at our website: avaandcarol.com

We hope you enjoyed reading the first book in the *Ava & Carol Detective Agency* series! Please leave a review on Amazon, Goodreads, or Barnes & Noble, we'd love to hear from you!

Find out what happens when Ava and Carol travel to Italy and witness an abduction. Order *The Mystery of Solomon's Ring* now so you don't miss out!

"Sending Ava & Carol off to Italy provides a vivid new backdrop, some REALLY memorable new characters, and a lot of fascinating history and tourism backdrops to explore. Plus, the girls' characters really continue to develop in this book, and they become more endearing on every page. Two thumbs way up!"

If you're looking for a fantastical adventure, you can enjoy the much-loved series of *Quest Chasers*.

"As a Harry Potter superfan, I could tell that this book would be a winner from just the cover. I loved the representation of Eevie and I aspired to be like her. Tommy is very funny and never failed to make me laugh. It was hard to keep a straight face."

If you love Darren Shan's series, then you'll enjoy *The Ghosts of Ian Stanley*. Great for teenagers who enjoy reading paranormal mysteries.

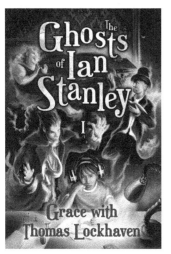

"I loved it so much it was a shame when it ended, I want more of it and yea it's a kid's book, don't be put off by that, it's still a good read even for an adult"

Learn about new book releases by following Thomas Lockhaven on Amazon and Goodreads, or visit our website at twistedkeypublishing.com.